LAST BATTLES

Machine gun bullets could not harm the Tiger, now arrogantly destroying the British vehicles as it cruised along the column...

In the market square personnel carriers were driven into side streets to clear the area and on the road the vehicles were halted awaiting further orders.

Just below the crest of Point 213 commanders were making frantic efforts to bring their vehicles out of the confusion all round them and to get them into action.

Wittmann saw them and appreciated the threat which they might pose. He decided to switch targets.

"Woll. Ahead of us just below the crest. The vehicles there at the head of the column. Range 400 metres. Destroy them..." The traversing gear swung the 88 away from the AFVs in the centre of the column and menaced those at its head.

"On" called the No 1 on the gun.

"Fire" and Woll's hand pressed the firing button.

Available in the Jackboot Series:

JB001	SS-Kampfgruppe Peiper	James Lucas
JB002	Death in Normandy	James Lucas

Forthcoming in the Jackboot Series:

JB003	Red Eagle	James Lucas

Death in Normandy

The Last Battles of Michael Wittmann

James Lucas

THIS IS FROM GERMAN
VIEW AND REALISTIC AND TRUE
FROM MY EXPERIENCE/

WITTMAN WAS THE GREATEST TANK
COMMANDER OF ANY ARMY AND IN
RUSSIA HAD DISPOSED OF 130 RUSSIAN
TANKS—
KNIGHTS CROSS WITH SWORDS AND
IRON CROSS FIRST CLASS

JACKBOOT SERIES 002

Published by SHELF BOOKS LTD
HALIFAX, WEST YORKSHIRE, UK

Published in the UK by Shelf Books Ltd, 1999

Revised and edited by J G Lewthwaite

Printed and Bound in the UK by Trafford Press, Manchester

Chapter 1

It was cool in the shade of the oaks. Out on the open hill it had been hot, the blinding August heat of Normandy that we remembered very clearly although forty years had passed since we fought here. Our group had been working on that shade-less hillside since sun-up but now it was midday and we were eating and resting. After lunch we would set out again, to work in that furnace heat, sweeping metal detectors across the ground until darkness fell or until we had found what we were looking for; the mortal remains of our former Company Commander, Michael Wittmann.

Under the great oaks we drank beer which had been cooled in the small stream running through the copse. The lunch was delicious but my mind was not on food. Time and again my eyes turned towards that shallow grassy slope on which, forty years ago to the day, Wittmann's Tiger tank Company had fought its last fight with him as its Commander. Somewhere, somewhere on that slight slope he had been lost. We did not even know for certain whether he had been killed and if he had indeed fallen in battle, how or exactly where this had happened. None in our Battalion who survived the War could remember in detail the events of that particular day. This is not as surprising as it sounds. To the soldier in action so much happens in so short a time that to him a single day's fighting is nothing more than a blur of impressions. All that was known for certain, when our Panzer Company pulled back at last light on 8th August, 1944, was that the battlefield was littered with the wrecks of knocked-out tanks and covered with the bodies of those who had fallen in action. We believed that Michael Wittmann was among the dead, but we could not be certain because his body had never been found and he was, therefore, listed as 'missing, believed killed.'

After the War the German War Graves Commission and then the SS Old Comrades' Association had begun their searches and had continued them until the late '60s, but had then given up. But we, his Battalion comrades, were still resolved. We had come to Normandy determined to find Wittmann and to give him a known and honourable grave. We intended to succeed where the others had failed. Don't ask me why we thought we could find him when they had not. We just did. This year the members of our ex-Service group had taken their summer holiday at the same time so that the individual and fruitless searches that we had each made at some time or another could be concentrated into one controlled and major effort. If our search did not find Wittmann, then nobody would.

We had begun work at first light on 8th August, but the result of more than five hours work had produced nothing more than a great many cartridge cases, a German waterbottle, an SS belt buckle and a mass of miscellaneous fragments of metal that might be bomb casings or pieces of tank armour. Nothing else.

During lunch we passed round sketches which had been drawn by survivors of the battle. On the most detailed were the outlines of a number of Tigers showing where each had been knocked out. Two machines lay to the south of the narrow road which runs towards St Aignan de Cramesnil and two others to the north of that track. Wittmann's panzer, No 007, was one of the pair to the south of the narrow road and had been destroyed, according to the sketch maps, some distance from the main Falaise-Caen road. The German War Graves people had cleared that part of France in the immediate post-war years but had found no bodies in the wreck of the panzer nor any close by it.

"Right comrades. On your feet."

Beck, our group leader, was calling us back to the task and the heat of early afternoon engulfed us as we moved out of the shade. I looked at my comrades as they made their slow way uphill. Did they see me as I saw them? Thick-waisted, grey-haired grandfathers whose common bonds were loyalty to a unit which had vanished into history and to comrades who had fallen in battle four decades earlier. It was because of those mystic concepts of loyalty and comradeship that we were here. Now we were ageing men, rheumatic, chesty and bourgeois. But once - ah!! Once we had been the standard bearers of a revolution; once, oh so many years ago.

~

The site where Tiger 007 had been destroyed was easy to find. When Wittmann's panzer blew up, the heavy turret, flung off by the force of the explosion, had landed upside down and had made a very deep indentation in the soft soil. The battlefield debris, the smashed tanks and carriers, had long since been taken away, but even after the forty years of ploughing and reaping the outline of that turret could still be seen in the ground. We swept round the 'kill' site again. The detectors identified metal. We dug again and again but found only more battlefield debris. All afternoon we swept the site, digging out and removing everything that registered and examining it closely, until at last the metal detectors registered nothing. But we had not found Wittmann nor any trace of a body. Late in the afternoon we moved away from the site, quartered the ground around it and swept - and found nothing. Then we circled the area, extending the radius from the indented earth, moving out in wide circles, sweeping with our detectors and digging when they registered metal. And found nothing.

It was well past four in the afternoon when work was halted for the day. We were all elderly and only the dedication of our special comradeship had kept us to the task for that length of time and in that heat. Silent and despondent we walked from where Tiger 007 had blown up towards the Caen road. Brodski was in the lead. Suddenly he stopped and pointed at a thick, wide hedge which bordered the road and whose growth almost hid from sight a grassy mound some two metres long but so low that it was almost level with the ground around it.

"Do you think?," he began. He did not need to say more. Our memories went back to battlefield burials we had experienced. That insignificant mound could well have been once a couple of slit trenches. After a battle such trenches were ready-made graves into which the unresisting dead would be tipped when there was neither time nor the inclination to inter them with fitting respect. Some of us pulled back the thick, concealing foliage while others prepared the sweeping equipment. Immediately, there were positive reactions. In that two metre length of earth there was buried metal - a lot of it and in several separate places.

"Stand back, comrades."

Beck was not only the group leader but, more importantly, he was with the German War Graves Commission. He was authorised to exhume. We were not. Obediently we stood back. Beck knelt down and despite his 65 years dug skilfully, carefully and swiftly, using the standard German Army entrenching tool. The turf layer was taken off. He sat back on his heels, sweating and breathless with the effort.

"Beer," he called. An opened bottle was handed over to him to be drunk in single, long swallow. "Back to work," he ordered himself and returned to the task. Then he called for a detector again.

Brodski swept the area and soon pinpointed a spot which gave off maximum reaction. The shining blade of the entrenching tool dug into the Norman soil and quickly turned up something which glistened white. A quick inspection was enough. It was part of a human shin bone. Beck dug more slowly, more carefully now and turned up bone fragments of a second body, then pieces of uniform and, finally, an identity tag. He handed it over his shoulder. After washing and some brisk rubbing a number was revealed. We checked our unit's nominal roll and there against the Service number was the name 'Hirschel'. He had been a comrade from the 101st and, more importantly, he had been in Wittmann's crew on that day. Next Beck uncovered the shattered skeleton of a third man. This one had no identity tag but his uniform was German. Beck explained to us that from the position of the bones this one had been thrown into the grave face downwards. A 6.34mm pistol in a rotting holster carried in the fabric of what had been a tunic pocket. The Tommies who had clearly flung the bodies into the trench had done this with such haste that they had not gone through the pockets. Wittmann had carried such a pistol of that calibre and with growing excitement we watched Beck's fingers ease the soil from around the skull. His fingers probed into the earth and then he held up an identity tag. Eager hands took it. It was washed in water and then dried on a handkerchief. Brodski looked at it, rubbed his eyes, looked again, then he read out a number. Fingers traced down the pages of the nominal roll. Then, from the circle of men a voice thick with emotion announced.

"Comrades. We have found our Company Commander."

In the grave two more bodies were found. One had no tag but the disc of the fifth man bore the number of Scharführer Heinrich Reimers. This was another of our Battalion and he too had been a member of Wittmann's crew on that last mission. There was also an MG42 in the grave. It was clear that the slit trenches had once been a machine gun position and that the unknown men buried there had been Grenadiers from the 'Hitler Youth' Division which we had been supporting. Tenderly, we covered all the skeleton pieces with turf and left them. At the inn Beck would telephone his colleagues in the War Grave office and report what we had found. They would send a burial detail to remove the fragments from their anonymous graves at the side of the Normandy road. An attempt would be made at positive identification by forensic tests after which the bones would be interred with full military honours in an official German War Cemetery.

Our search had been successful. Don't ask me why the searchers in earlier years had not found that slit trench grave. But they had not. The reasons for their failure did not concern us. The fact remains we had found Michael Wittmann and I lay unsleeping for a long time in the silence of the night, kept awake not only by the emotion of the find we had made but because I have been an insomniac since I lost my leg.

Lying there in the dark my mind went back to the battles of that Summer of 1944. My brain projected onto the white-washed ceiling of the bedroom, images as clear as photographic slides and I saw again the high green walls of the bocage which hemmed in the Tommies, but whose cover we had been taught to exploit. There were smells in my nose. Not the perfume of roses and honeysuckle from the garden of the inn but the stink of oil and cordite, of petrol and sweat - the aromas of a panzer man. It was no longer soft bedclothes that I could feel but cold unyielding armour plate. My left leg throbbed and pained as it had, so many years ago, when it was smashed and had had to be amputated. My brain pulsed as rhythmically as a panzer engine and rising above that dull beat there sounded in my mind, clearly and exultantly, the Panzer song that we had once sung with such confidence. And I wept silently in the night. Not just for the comrades whom I had lost, nor because of the pain of my amputation, but for my lost youth and vigour. Wittmann had been lucky. He had fallen at the peak of his fame. The most successful panzer commandant in the history of tank warfare had died in combat. Not for him the humiliation of surrender in May 1945, nor the years of imprisonment in the hell camps of the Soviet Union, but a quick, clean, soldier's death in the pride of an August day.

In those hours of darkness and pain, lying there in the bedroom of the inn, I reflected on what I remembered about our Company Commander, on what those who had known him well had told me and what the propaganda people of the time had written about him. With those memories in my mind it was hard to relate that earth-encrusted skull in the roadside grave to the living man whom I had known.

A question nagged persistently and gave me no peace. Why had Wittmann and his crew been buried nearly half a kilometre away from their Tiger? The Tommies would not have carried them that far but would have tipped all the dead into the nearest deep hole or trench. If German soldiers had interred them then this would have been carried out more neatly and someone would have taken off the lower half of the identity tags. The question nagged me as I lay in the dark, why were the graves so far from the panzer? I decided to try and resolve it.

The result of my research is this book which contains all our group's collected recollections of the battle in Normandy and what we remember of our Commander's part in it. These, together with official German records such as war diaries and post-battle reports as well as contributions from those allied soldiers against whom we had once fought, as opponents but never as enemies, will, I hope, complete the record of Michael Wittmann, holder of the Knight's Cross with Oak Leaves and Swords, Hauptsturmführer of the Waffen SS and commander of No 2 Company of 101st SS Heavy Panzer Battalion.

Chapter 2

The voice at the Normandy terminal of the telephone link was curt and impatient.

"I don't give a damn what you say cannot be done," the voice snapped out. "I order you to wake Jodl. He must tell the Führer that the invasion has begun."

"With respect," replied a tremulous voice at the Berchtesgaden terminal, "The Colonel General is asleep. The Führer conference finished only a short time ago…"

"Are you all bloody mad up there? I'll explain it in simple terms so that even you can understand. The Allies have begun their invasion. Their paratroops are falling from the sky and the whole damned sea is covered with their ships…thousands of ships. Their armour is moving inland. Do you understand? You do? Then for God's sake wake Jodl and tell him what I have just told you. Without Hitler's authority we here in Normandy cannot move the two Panzer Divisions which are held in Supreme Command reserve and launch them into a counter-attack. Do you understand that? Well, then wake Jodl and get those Divisions released." The voice at the Normandy terminal suddenly became cold and menacing.

"Listen, you dolt. If we do not put those two Panzer Divisions into action within a couple of hours the Allies will have gained a firm beachhead. They will burst out of that one day and we shall lose Normandy. And if we lose Normandy, then we lose France, then will follow the Low Countries and finally we shall have lost the War." Then came a whiplash snap; the rasping voice of a Prussian barely holding his temper in check. "I am giving you a direct order. Wake that oaf Jodl and tell him."

But the nervous subordinate of the irascible Chief of Staff of OKW, the Oberkommando der Wehrmacht, the Armed Forces High Command, did not dare waken him. Instead he telephoned Hitler's house, the Berghof, in Berchtesgaden. Janko von Puttkamer, the Führer's Naval Liaison Officer was on duty and took the call. He noted the time in the duty log; 0500hrs precisely. Patiently he listened to the flood of words and waited until there was a pause.

"May I put a question?," he interjected.

"Yes, of course," came the reply.

"How do you know," asked Puttkamer, "that it is the real invasion and not just a feint attack? You don't. Well then, you cannot expect me to wake the Führer because of every rumour that is noised abroad.

Even if your report is true there is little that he can do to influence the battle, at this early stage - is there?"

It was at this point that Jodl's nervous aide should have, but did not, mention the release of the two Panzer Divisions as a matter of priority. Instead he repeated what he had told by the voice at the Normandy terminal in the headquarters of Supreme Commander West, that the cross-Channel invasion had come in. Puttkamer again waited politely for the aide to stop talking.

"Is there anything else?" he asked. "No? Just the invasion rumour? Well, thank you and goodbye. You may depend upon it. I shall lay the information before the Führer when he wakes at noon."

Jodl's aide would not wake him and because von Puttkamer remained unconvinced that the assault in Normandy was the principal allied invasion, Hitler was not woken immediately. The fate of the German armies defending Normandy thus depended upon the sleeping habits of its most senior commanders and upon the cowardice of one aide de camp and the opinion of another. And both Puttkamer, the Führer's Naval Liaison Officer and Jodl's aide had been wrong. The invasion had begun and it was the main attack and the voice at the Normandy terminal had been correct. His statement had accorded with all the facts; with all the messages that were pouring into the headquarters of the field armies just as they had been pouring in since just after midnight.

The first had been at 0030hrs, Central European Time, when No 5 Company of 125th Panzergrenadier Regiment, out on a night exercise near the coast, passed a wireless message to battalion that enemy paratroops were being dropped. That report was passed to 21st Panzer Division whose Ic forwarded it, together with similar ones from other companies of the battalion, one of which had captured the first British prisoners of war - men of 6th Airborne Division.

Only a few hours later reports came in of heavy air raids and then, at 0500hrs, the guns of the allied naval armada had opened up. Covered by that fire the landings had begun and ninety minutes later the first swimming Shermans reached the beaches and began to roll inland. And yet, and yet - despite all the available evidence there were many German senior commanders who could not and would not accept that this was the long-awaited cross-Channel invasion of Western Europe. One reason for their disbelief was that, according to their logical minds, the Allies had landed in the wrong place. A second reason was that for those officers to have admitted that this was the invasion would have been to contradict the Führer. He had stated that the Anglo-Americans would choose the short sea route and that, consequently, their armies would debark on beaches in the Pas de Calais area. His opinion was shared by Speidel, Rommel's Chief of Staff at Army Group B who as late as 1710hrs on the afternoon of D-Day, reported his collected impressions to the Operations Department of OKW. He dismissed the landings as "a major enemy undertaking, which does not exclude a far greater enemy undertaking..." In other words the landings in Normandy were likely to be a bluff - a diversionary attack to cover the REAL assault which would be made somewhere else, and most likely in the Pas de Calais.

With hindsight and with records from the archives of all the protagonists, we can see that the conflicting opinions of senior German commanders led to mistakes being made on the way in which they planned to meet the invasion, and how those plans would be carried out. The first and most fundamental difference of opinion was between von Rundstedt, the Supreme Commander West and his subordinate, Rommel, the Commander-in-Chief of Army Group B. Rommel, the 'Desert Fox' had the greater experience of fighting against the Anglo-Americans. He had fought them first in the deserts of Libya, then in the mountains of Tunisia, in the island of Sicily and, finally, in the mud of Italy. Rommel's plan was to smash the invaders as they approached the shores of Normandy, for he had concluded that it was there that the allies would land. He was determined to crush their assault on the beaches and well before the Anglo-Americans were able to land in great numbers. And to do this he demanded that the Panzer Divisions be brought well forward so that they could be launched into action with minimal delay.

Von Rundstedt, the Supreme Commander West, had no recent campaign experience against the Western Allies, but he was the better strategist. He was unconvinced that the allies would land in Normandy. To his trained mind the Anglo-Americans needed a large port and must, therefore, choose the short route and land in the Calais/Boulogne area. As a compromise between Calais and Normandy he did propose that the panzer force should be concentrated in the dense woods around Paris, ready to be deployed, once the allied intention was clear, either northwards to Calais or south-westwards to Normandy. He would then, while the newly-arrived Allied armies were still unprepared and unready for a set piece battle, fling against them the massed panzer force of his Command and destroy them utterly. He was not concerned with deflecting a sea-borne landing which might be launched in a matter of months. His strategy was to destroy the enemy forces which had landed so completely that the allies would not be able to make another attempt for years. To achieve that victory he needed to keep the Panzer Divisions well back from the landing beaches to be launched en masse once the allied 'Schwerpunkt', the area of the REAL invasion had been established.

Hitler, to whom both commanders appealed, would make no decision but compromised and deployed some of the Panzer Divisions so that they would operate in the way that von Rundstedt had proposed while leaving others to be disposed so that they would act according to Rommel's strategy. As a brake upon the impetuous Rommel, Hitler ordered that two Panzer Divisions which were under the command of Rommel's Army Group B were to be detached and placed in the OKW reserve. Thereby, the decision whether, or when, to release the Divisions was his alone and it was the Führer's decision which the voice at the Normandy terminal had demanded.

This work, however, is not a history of Command decisions, but of warfare as fought by those of us who lived because of our skill or luck or died for lack of those attributes. In this story of Michael Wittmann in Normandy, I shall deal with one of those two formations in the OKW reserve; 12th SS Panzer Division 'Hitler Youth', as well as the 101st SS Heavy Panzer Battalion in which Wittmann was a Company commander and in which we had also served. His Company was detached from our Battalion to serve with the 12th SS, and specifically with the 25th SS Panzergrenadier Regiment. The period which is dealt with in this narrative is from just before D-Day, 6th June to 8th August, when Wittmann fell in action.

The story of Wittmann and of the 'Hitler Youth' Division in Normandy begins with the failure to release the 12th SS Panzer Division 'Hitler Youth' in time for it to undertake a swift and massive counter-attack against the Allied beachhead. The voice at the Normandy terminal had demanded this but it had not been the first. As early as 0445hrs on the morning of D-Day, even before the sea-borne landings began, other officers in the office of von Rundstedt, the Supreme Commander West had telephoned and had asked for both Divisions to be released from OKW reserve but the Supreme Commander, Hitler and his Chief of Staff were asleep and Jodl's aide would not risk waking his superior because of a rumour. To cover his cowardice, or if we are charitable, his inaction, the Chief of Staff's nervous aide, using the 'old boy' network had telephoned friends and learned from them that the allied invasion was reality and not rumour. Their confirmations steeled him into making the decision to wake the Colonel General. The awakened Jodl put through a telephone call to the Führer's military adjutant, General Schmundt, telling him that air and sea landings were being made along the Cotentin peninsula. Schmundt then telephoned Hitler's valet, Linge, asking to speak to the Führer on an urgent matter. Linge woke Hitler who discussed the situation with Schmundt. Nothing was said by the aide to Jodl - nor by Jodl to Schmundt - nor by Schmundt to Hitler about the urgent need to release the two Panzer Divisions and the Führer, being unaware of the urgency, did not issue the order to release them. The two Divisions stayed in position and, therefore, inactive, while only a handful of kilometres from them allied soldiers, guns and armoured fighting vehicles streamed off the beaches and fanned out into the Normandy bocage.

Independence of thought and freedom of action were basic concepts to the officers who served on the German General Staff. They were not appointed in order to serve as the rubber stamps of their superiors but were expected, indeed required, to act on their own initiative. Four years of war; four years of the Führer's interference in High Command matters had diminished but not totally destroyed those concepts, so that General Wohlgemuth serving in the headquarters of Supreme Commander West and acting on behalf of his superior, von Rundstedt, had used the prerogative of independence and passed a message to Panzer Group West which read,

"Without affecting its position as part of OKW reserve, 12th SS Panzer Division 'Hitler Youth' is hereby directed to send out a reconnaissance detachment to the sector where 711th Infantry Division is positioned; is to gain touch with that Division and must also be prepared to act against possible enemy airlandings in the area."

Wohlgemuth had acted independently, but not so independently as to commit the whole of the 'Hitler Youth' Division to battle. There was, after all, little point in stirring up a hornet's nest at the Führer's headquarters by an act of major disobedience, but a minor one might be excused, overlooked or even possibly approved. From the headquarters of Supreme Commander West to Panzer Group West and then to 1st SS Panzer Corps the order was passed. Then from Dietrich's Corps headquarters to the 'Hitler Youth' Division and finally from that Division to its Reconnaissance Battalion.

Chapter 3

"Obersturmführer," the voice of the Duty NCO was urgent and insistent as he shook his Company Commander into wakefulness. "Message from Battalion. The invasion has begun. The CO told me to say this is not, repeat not, an exercise. The Tommies have landed. The CO wants to speak to you on the telephone."

Outside in the dark night somebody began ringing the Company alarm bell and overlying that high-pitched clanging came a heavy droning; the sound that every soldier in the German Army in the West knew full well. It was the sound of aircraft engines, of allied air fleets flying out on a bombing mission. The young Obersturmführer hastened, bare-footed, through the grass to the Company office, blinking as he entered from the darkness of the night into the well-lit room. He spoke into the mouthpiece of the field telephone.

"Sturmbannführer?"

"Richter? Listen. The invasion is on. Assemble a group of ten armoured cars and two troops of motor cyclists. Report to me here in 30 minutes."

"What about the remainder of the Company, Sturmbannführer?"

"They are to dress ready for action but are to remain in their quarters until they are called for."

The oft-repeated night exercises and the battle drill rehearsals which had dominated the past weeks had been no waste of time. Well before the allowed half hour had passed Obersturmführer Richter was reporting to Gerd Bremer, the Reconnaissance Battalion Commander, to receive his orders for the recce patrol. He returned to his men standing by their armoured cars.

"Gather round, lads. You must all know by now that the invasion has begun. The 711th Division is holding positions close to the coast where the Tommies have dropped paratroops. We are to carry out a recce to see what the situation is like on 711's sector." He looked round the circle of faces only half visible in the pale moonlight. "As a recce unit it is our job to see but not to be seen. So make sure we aren't seen. Another thing. Watch the road verges for mines. Those damned terrorists, the so-called Resistance fighters may have laid some. They'll probably snipe at us as well. If we are fired on we return fire. Right. Mount up, ready to march in five minutes."

He had barely finished speaking when Standartenführer Meyer - Panzermeyer - Commander of 25th SS Panzergrenadier Regiment swung into the farm courtyard on a motor cycle. On the pillion seat was Bremer, the Recce Battalion Commander.

"Ready to march, Richter?"

"Yes, Sturmbannführer."

"Standartenführer Meyer would like to go with you. That is, if you have no objection."

"An honour, Sturmbannführer," replied the young officer stiffly and unenthusiastically. He had been looking forward to his leading his own men in their first action. Now Panzermeyer, as the senior officer, would lead the group. Meyer sensed the junior officer's disappointment.

"I am coming only as an observer, Richter. You are in command."

"Thank you, Standartenführer. Will you ride in an armoured car?"

"Thank you, no. I prefer my motor cycle. Ready? Let's go."

Richter swung himself over the turret rim of his 8 wheeled armoured car and picked up the intercom microphone. "Panzer Marsch. Speed 40kms." The mission had begun.

Panzermeyer rode with the lead group of motor cyclists. Behind that first detachment were the four-wheeled and eight-wheeled armoured cars and then the second group of motor cyclists. The column was well spread out, fifty metres distance between each armoured car, as a precaution against allied fighter-bomber attacks. It was not yet dawn and the allied Jabos would not yet be in the air, but keeping distance even at night was a good discipline. The patrol drove through the warm June night, through villages whose inhabitants still slept, unaware that on the nearby coast history was being made. There were neither mines in the road verges nor snipers in the trees. It must be, thought the young officer, still too early for the Resistance to be up and about, even though the sky was beginning to lighten. Dawn of 6th June, 1944, would soon break.

A fast and uninterrupted drive brought the recce group at about 6 in the morning into the western suburbs of Caen. The young officer decided to rest his men for a break before undertaking the final drive to the coast. They stood around their vehicles eating food which the unit cooks had prepared before they set out again. Suddenly Panzermeyer stopped eating and looked up.

"Hear that?" he asked. "That's heavy artillery. The Tommies could not have brought their heavies ashore so quickly. Of course," he struck his forehead with the palm of his hand. "Of course. It's naval artillery and the sound is coming from the sector which the 711th is holding. I pity them if the Tommies are bombarding the area with their heavy battleships."

He turned back to face the Obersturmführer.

"Do you know that cafe opposite? Yes? What is it called?"

"It is the Café Verdun, Standartenführer."

"And the name of this suburb?"

"St Germain la Blanche Herbe."

"Is the cafe open?"

"I don't know, but if it isn't we can soon make sure that it is. Do you want a drink, Standartenführer?"

"Yes. I fancy a Calvados. It is the local fire-water, isn't it?"

"No need to go into the cafe. I have a bottle in the armoured car."

Panzermeyer drank the fiery liquid straight from the bottle in long slow swallows.

"It's good stuff. Made of apples, isn't it.?" and without waiting for Richter's answer went on, "We'd better press on soon. I don't want to usurp your authority but the allied fighter-bombers will be active now that it is daylight and I want to report back to Div HQ as soon as possible my assessment of the situation in the landing areas."

The speed of the column was increased to 80kph and Richter ordered the drivers to keep as close as they could to the side of the road in order to gain some cover from the allied aircraft. Within minutes of giving the order came the cry 'Jabos'. The column halted under the roadside trees and waited while RAF Typhoons flew low up and down the ruler-straight road searching for victims but finding none. The pilots had not seen the recce column drawn up under the trees and climbed away to patrol another sector.

"Panzer Marsch," and the detachment moved off but within minutes - fighter-bombers were reported again. Another halt and then Richter made a decision. At the next junction the column would leave the main road and drive along country lanes. Their high bocage hedges would afford sufficient overhead cover to protect the vehicles against being seen by the Spitfires and Typhoons. The young officer realised that a diversion through minor roads would add to the length of the drive but he knew it was a sensible precaution. Orders were passed by wireless to the armoured cars and by arm signals to the motor cyclists. The column swung off the main road and wound its way through narrow twisting lanes whose gradients became steeper as the road neared the coast. The column passed through the deserted hamlet of St Sulpice, which from its desolate air had obviously been evacuated by its inhabitants. St Sulpice was undamaged but to the left of the column, in the village of Tracy, houses were on fire and huge columns of earth and smoke rose up as heavy shells crashed down and exploded in its streets. Moving more slowly now and with every sense alert, the recce group drove to just below the ridge near Magny en Bessin. From its crest there was a panoramic view of the bay of Arromanches. When the Obersturmführer reached him Panzermeyer was already lying prone on the ground by the side of a barn and was checking the bustling movement below him through powerful binoculars.

"Scharführer Rolf," called Richter. The young NCO clicked his heels.

"Obersturmführer?"

"Get the vehicles under cover and make sure they are properly camouflaged. Then get in touch with Div HQ. I'll need a clear line to make my report."

"Obersturmführer," the NCO responded and hurried away to supervise the camouflaging of the armoured cars with scrim nets and tree branches.

On the ground Meyer was swearing softly to himself, astounded - no shocked - at the masses of men and materials that were gathering on the beach, that were moving inland from the beach and which were landing on the beach from an armada of landing craft. The inexperienced Obersturmführer did not see the scene below in the way that the veteran commander saw it.

"What is that grey wall out there about a kilometre from shore," he asked. "I can't make it out through my binoculars."

"Ships," replied Panzermeyer bitterly. "Hundreds, possibly thousands of ships."

"But that wall stretches from the eastern to the western horizon. They can't all be ships"

"Oh, yes they can. The enemy has all the ships he needs. After all it takes a great mass of vessels to take the allied armies to fight. The Anglo-Americans," declared the Standartenführer even more bitterly, "do not fight in their own countries but are shipped overseas to fight in other people's countries...Do you see that...there...over there...They've got swimming tanks?"

"All I can see are the tanks landing from those big vessels," replied Richter, "Swimming tanks as well? Tell me, Standartenführer, you have years of combat experience. Have you ever seen anything on this scale before?"

"On this scale, no. The Russians often put in whole Tank armies for a major offensive, but numbers like this," he shook his head. "Such numbers I have never seen."

Both officers continued to check the beaches, sweeping their binoculars from Arromanches in the west towards the Orne river in the east.

"Richter. I must ask a favour of you. Please don't misunderstand me but if you report over the radio what you have seen, there are some at Div HQ who will put down your estimates of enemy strengths to the exaggerations of a lad who had not yet been shot over. Do you understand?" The young officer nodded in agreement. Panzermeyer was right, of course. The Regimental Commander's report would carry weight. No one at Div would accuse Panzermeyer of exaggeration if he reported what he had seen. The Regimental Commander climbed into Richter's armoured car.

"Are we on Div frequency?" he asked the wireless operator.

"Yes, Standartenführer."

Slowly and in precise detail Panzermeyer first described what he had seen on the beaches and then gave his assessment of the situation ending with:

"It is clear that the Tommies are heading for the airfield at Carpiquet. If our Division, the H J, moves now we can not only hold them but could even drive them back into the sea. Well," he asked eagerly, "have we and the Panzer Lehr Division been released from OKW control? Not yet? Well, when will the Führer release us?" Suddenly his eyes widened in surprise at what he had been told over the radio. It was a surprise which was echoed in his voice. "When he wakes up? Are you telling me that no-one has woken the Führer to tell him?"

He listened intently and then spoke again. "So, while Adolf is having a good sleep we have got to sit on our fat arses and watch our enemies landing under our very noses...Heads should roll for this bloody stupidity." He stopped abruptly and when he spoke again his voice was respectful and subdued.

"Yes, Gruppenführer. Yes. I realise that what I have said was treasonable..." then anger swept over him again,"...but so is what is happening here at Arromanches. Permission to return, Gruppenführer? Thank you," and then turning round in the turret he shouted down to Richter. "Let's go home and tell those donkeys at Div what we have seen..." and then went on in a sad voice. "By God, but I do despair sometimes..."

The drivers took off the scrim netting, reversed their vehicles with considerable difficulty in the narrow lane and soon the column was heading back to the concentration area of the 'Hitler Youth' Division, south west of Caen.

Chapter 4

The location and timing of the allied invasion created, to begin with, a certain doubt among the Command staffs of the German Army in the West until training and experience reasserted themselves and counter-measures began to be taken. The doubt expressed at senior Command level was whether the landings were real or just a feint. Either way divisions and corps would have to be moved. There would have to be a great deal of re-deployment and the code words ordering units to be at instant readiness to move were issued to all formations, even to those in the OKW reserve. Those senior officers on the staff of Supreme Commander West who expected the invasion to be made in the Calais area, remained unconvinced of the genuineness of the Normandy landings and prepared to move 7th Army and Panzer Group West northwards so as to support 15th Army when the REAL allied landings they expected were made in the Pas de Calais. Those commanders who were of the other opinion and who were convinced that the Normandy invasion was 'on', began checking routes and concentration areas in which the divisions of 15th Army would be located when they were detached to support the armies in Normandy. There was another group of leaders; men who had not expected that the invasion would come in when it did. Field Marshal Rommel, Commander of Army Group B, was one of these. He had been of the opinion that the weather was too bad for the Allies to sail and had gone home on leave.

And overall, affecting the planning in all the senior Command headquarters in the West, hung the realisation that until the Führer woke and made a decision any preparations which the staff officers had begun could not be activated. Nevertheless, in the same way that General Wohlgemuth had acted on his own initiative in the matter of sending out recce patrols from the 12th SS Panzer Division, so had other staff officers acted and had prepared their formations to meet whichever of the two options, Normandy or Calais, proved to be the correct one. This intelligent anticipation on the part of those officers had begun in the earliest hours of D-Day, but it is Wohlgemuth's decisions which are of interest to us for he had not only sent out the reconnaissance patrol but had acted on the information it had brought back and had issued the code word which set the 'Hitler Youth' moving from its original concentration areas to new ones around Bernay-Lisieux-Vimoutiers.

At about the time that Panzermeyer and Richter were driving

towards the invasion beaches at Arromanches, Michael Wittmann, Commander of No 2 Company of 101st SS Heavy Panzer Battalion was breakfasting with the Battalion Commander, Sturmbannführer von Westerhagen.

The 101st was a Tiger tank battalion and like all such formations was not subordinated to a particular division but was at the disposal of the Corps Commander who deployed not only the Battalion but at times even individual Companies of the Battalion, to act as a battering ram in an attack or to form a solid rock in a defensive situation. The Tiger was so heavily armoured that it was practically indestructible by allied tank guns, except at close range, whereas its own main armament, the powerful 88mm gun, could 'kill' a victim at ranges up to and even above 2kms.

The 101st, as part of the OKW reserve and subordinate to von Rundstedt's strategy, lay at Beauvais, outside Paris. At a table set in a quiet orchard of a convent von Westerhagen and his subordinate sat and ate and discussed the reports of the invasion.

"What you are asking, Michael," said von Westerhagen at length "is permission to go into the area held by the 'Hitler Youth' Division and to 'sniff the air' so to speak."

"Yes, Sturmbannführer. That is my intention. I'd like to look over the ground. The terrain there is, I understand, quite unlike that in this part of France and that will mean a change of tactics, among other things."

"You realise" asked the Sturmbannführer "that we are in OKW reserve and might be moved at any time?"

"Certainly."

"And we don't yet know if this Normandy thing is the actual invasion or just a Tommy bluff. We might be moved down into Normandy or, on the other hand, the Battalion may be put into action around Calais."

"It would present no problem, Sturmbannführer" Wittmann assured his superior. "It's an evens bet, isn't it? And if the 101st goes to the Pas de Calais, it would not take me long to rejoin it. If it is ordered to march to Normandy, well, then I shall be already there."

"Very good, Michael. Go down to the 'Hitler Youth', if you've a mind to. Keep your eyes open and let us know what you think of the Tommies' and the Amis' methods of making war. They are an unknown quantity to most of us in the Division. Only those who fought the Tommies in Greece in 1941, know how they fought, so your impressions would be of value. Right. You may go on your swan around Normandy."

Wittmann left Beauvais and hurtled down the southwards leading roads on a motor cycle. A stop at Corps HQ would not only give him a chance to rest and eat, but from Sturmbannführer Kraemer, the Chief of Staff, he could get the latest information. The Chief of Staff was studying the map on the wall of his office, pointing out details of movements to a short, burly man who stood facing him, hands on hips, legs spread wide apart. Wittmann recognised him at once. This was Sepp Dietrich, the Corps Commander. Kraemer stopped talking as Wittmann entered the room and the Obersturmführer, realising that he was intruding, saluted and turned to leave.

"Don't go, Wittmann," Kraemer called out. "We are discussing the latest sitreps." He waved the bundle of situation reports and wireless messages which had come in to Corps HQ. "Come here," he continued. "This is an education in monumental confusion."

Wittmann walked over to his superiors, shook hands with them both and looked at the marked-up map hanging on the wall. From the Belgian border to the Mediterranean there were the standard blue markings indicating German units, but then his eyes turned towards Normandy and there, like a rash of chicken pox, were red dots and lines covering the base of the Cotentin peninsula and extending eastwards as far as the Orne river.

"Confusion?," he queried politely.

"Balls-up, more like" Sepp Dietrich had been an NCO in the Great War and his manner of speech showed it. "Them up there,-" his gesture towards the chateau ceiling embraced all senior officers up to and including the OKW. "Them up there are running about like headless chickens. They don't know which way to send us, so they keep us here and send no firm orders. Look here..." He jabbed a square finger at the map. Wittmann recognised the name of the small town as being the area in which 12th SS Division was to concentrate in the event of an allied landing.

"Some clever bastard," Dietrich continued "issued the code word which ordered the Division to move to the concentration area. It would have been from here that my lads in the 12th would have advanced to attack the Tommies..." 'Sepp' stopped to mop the back of his neck with a huge bandanna handkerchief. He pushed his peaked Service cap to the back of his balding head, looking for all the world like a caricature of a pre-war Drill Sergeant.

"At the last moment," Kraemer broke in, taking over the briefing, "Panzer Group West changed the location of the concentration area and while the units were en route to that second venue there came another change. This time the Division is to concentrate to the south-west of Caen. Of course, its still under OKW - so is Panzer Lehr Division, by the way, so God alone knows when both of us will be released to make our move." He paused and stood morosely staring at the map.

"Sturmbannführer," Wittmann broke in. "You said that the 'Hitler Youth' is en route to positions to the south-west of Caen. Where exactly?"

"Well, some units are to group round Messy; down here," he used a pointer to show its location. "But if I were you, I'd head for Caen and look out for unit markers. The Division will be sure to blaze the trail for late arrivals."

"By the by, Wittmann," Dietrich asked "You haven't told us what you are doing here. You're not swanning about, are you? The situation is too grave for that sort of nonsense."

"No, Obergruppenführer. Once we are committed to battle, my Company will be supporting part of the 12th SS. I was going down to re-establish contact with old friends and to make my number known among the new lads."

"How do you know we will be deployed in Normandy? If you know that then you're cleverer than the Army clowns at Supreme Command West."

"I don't know, Obergruppenführer, but if it is Calais, well, I know that area, its tactical advantages and the disadvantages. The Normandy bocage is an unknown factor and as I explained to Sturmbannführer von Westerhagen, I should like to familiarise myself with the terrain."

"Have you eaten anything since lunch?"

"No, but I shall go to the officers' Mess and have something there."

"Make sure you do, Wittmann. Never ride anything; a woman, a horse or a vehicle, on an empty stomach." He bellowed with laughter; a wheezy roar which filled the room. "Now that's a piece of advice that's worth a fortune."

Wittmann saluted, shook hands with both men and left. Pausing only to eat a light meal he set out again for Caen. When he arrived the town was in an uproar. Wave after wave of allied bombers had attacked it and fires were burning everywhere. Now that the allied aircraft had flown away the streets were filled with civilians, French policemen and firemen as well as men from every branch of the German armed forces all working at fever pitch to bring out from beneath the rubble those who were trapped in the collapsed buildings. A fractured gas pipe carried at its break a long blue flame, like a giant Bunsen burner. The scene of toiling bodies against a backdrop of flames was apocalyptic. Wittmann pulled his motor cycle to a place at the kerb and called to a soldier busily engaged in moving bricks by hand from around a deep crater.

"Do you know where the 'Hitler Youth' Division is located?"

The soldier straightened up, saw the rank badges and the Knights Cross. Snapping to attention he replied, "So far as I know, only parts of the Division have come up and they're out on the south-west road between here and Carpiquet. More than that I do not know, Obersturmführer."

"Thank you...When did all this happen?" asked Wittmann gesturing towards the destruction.

"It finished about half an hour ago. It was like the end of the world. I've never experienced anything like it. The allies bombed this place - I can't imagine why - and the people here are supposed to be on their side. Allies - some allies." He paused. "Excuse me, Obersturmführer, I have to go back. There's someone trapped under a beam near that crater."

Chapter 5

The confusion which had plagued the Command staffs during the morning of D-Day grew as orders, directions and instructions were passed down through the military hierarchy resulting in chaos as regimental units sought to obey each of several conflicting sets of orders they had received. The old Army advice, 'Obey the last order', was nonsense in a situation in which the last order was promptly cancelled and a replacement order issued.

In the course of the morning of 6th June, 1st SS Panzer Corps was informed that unfortunately, 'due to a breakdown in communications...' Supreme Command West had not been able to advise it that 12th SS Panzer Division 'Hitler Youth', had been ordered to concentrate in the Bernay-Lisieux-Vimoutiers area. Hard upon the receipt of that half-hearted apology had come the signal which, as we have seen, had upset 'Sepp' Dietrich and Kraemer, his Chief of Staff. That new signal from Supreme Commander West changed the location of the concentration area from Bernay to Evrecy some 9kms to the south west of Caen. It was not only the 'Hitler Youth' which had been treated in so cavalier a fashion. Indeed, it seemed as if all the divisions of Army Group B and Panzer Group West were being shunted around Normandy, seemingly without definite purpose or plan. While the German divisional formations were receiving confusing and contradictory orders, allied forces poured onto the French beaches and struck inland encountering little opposition from the shell-shocked remnants of the German coastal defence formations. Against the armadas of aircraft which the Allies launched into the air the Luftwaffe was able to put up, in the first hours of the invasion, only one single fighter plane. The German Navy's response to the challenge of D-Day was minimal.

The Allies had triumphed. They had hoodwinked the Nazis. Surprise had been complete, or so an objective observer might have thought. That was not the way Hitler viewed the situation. When he arrived at OKW for the lunch-time briefing, he declared the whole allied operation to be a bluff. The real blow MUST fall in the Pas de Calais. He knew this. How could he be wrong? He refused to be hurried into making a decision on troop deployments, so that it was not until 1430hrs that he issued the order releasing 12th SS and Panzer Lehr Divisions from OKW reserve and then, having at last released them, expected that they would go immediately into a victorious counter-attack. It was a tragedy that the limitations of time and space bedevilled even the operations launched by the self-proclaimed greatest military genius in the history of the world, It had to be pointed out to the Führer that it would be several hours before the Panzer Divisions which he had just set free could reach the form-up areas from which they would be able to begin to make their concerted assault. Reluctantly, he accepted the delay but gave orders that 12th SS should move forward to where 21st Panzer Division was already in the line and that both Divisions were to attack on the following day, 7th June, and that they were to sweep the allied invaders into the sea. Panzer Lehr, the other Division released from OKW reserve, was ordered to move to a new concentration area some 50kms to the south-west of Caen.

Hitler's demand for a concerted attack by 12th SS and 21st Panzer Divisions was an order which would be hard to execute; perhaps even impossible. Although the 21st Panzer was grouped and ready it could not go into the attack without the 'Hitler Youth' whose formations were strung out across Normandy and were not even in radio contact. There was a general order commanding the strictest wireless silence. As a result of that ban some formations of the 'Hitler Youth' were still heading for the Bernay-Vimoutiers concentration area while others were en route to Evrecy, south-west of Caen. Dispersed as they were across so wide an area of Normandy, there could be no question of them launching a concentrated divisional attack until they had been assembled and had been lined up for battle. To compound the confusion of which Dietrich and Kraemer had complained, Supreme Command West sent out a fresh signal ordering the Division to move towards the coastal sector, "...Seine estuary to east of the Orne estuary...," which 711th Division was defending. That order laid out the divisional route through Caen, and that meant a long and difficult detour for most units. Protests from SS Panzer Corps that the roads had not been recced were ignored. Supreme Command West demanded total compliance with its orders and regimental officers in the 12th SS protesting to Kraemer met only with the response, 'It is an order. Carry it out.' He knew and those officers knew that by ordering the 'Hitler Youth' Division to follow the route which had been ordered its columns would have to drive through a countryside over which a 'cab rank' of allied fighter bombers hung in menacing and death-dealing chains.

By 1700hrs in the afternoon of D-Day, there was total confusion in the headquarters of 12th SS. Three conflicting orders had been received each specifying a new concentration area. Order - counter order - disorder: The condemning formula remained unchanged and now the 'Hitler Youth' units were marching towards an as yet unknown battlefield from three different concentration areas. The only concrete information which the units had been told was that the enemy had dropped paratroops east of the Orne river and that a landing was taking place in Arromanches bay. The commanders of 12th SS prayed fervently that the Tommies had not advanced very far inland from the beaches. If they had, then the 12th SS would have to fight a full-scale battle while its units were on the move; always a confused affair. If, on the other hand, the enemy had not struck inland then their inaction would make easier the task of carrying out liaison with 21st Panzer Division before they both undertook the attack on the 7th. The commanders of the 'Hitler Youth' had trained their units to attack. The summer's day of 7th June would see the lads making an all out assault to fulfil the Führer's order to sweep the Tommies into the sea. .

Thanks to a fortunate weather situation during the morning of the 6th, as the Division's motorised columns began their drive across Normandy, they were untroubled by the Jabos, the fighter-bombers of the RAF's 2nd Tactical Air Force. Low cloud ceilings prevented the allied machines from operating. During the afternoon OKW capitalised upon that piece of meteorological good fortune by ordering all units to move fast along the main roads towards the beachhead. The immunity given by the low ceiling lasted until 1750hrs, but then the clouds broke and dispersed to disclose a summer evening of perfect visibility. Within minutes allied fighter bombers, called by radio to dream targets - vehicle columns on open roads - swept down and with rocket and machine gun inflicted death and destruction upon the SS.

"Bastards. Vicious bastards..." Panzermeyer's face was crimson with fury and his uniform was covered with dust. Riding at the head of 1st Battalion of his regiment, he had seen, as his Horch staff car turned a corner, that directly ahead along the road and only 500 metres distant stood an undamaged bridge across a small river. The question in Meyer's mind was how long would it remain intact and even as he considered that question the cry came over the vehicle radio, "Achtung. Achtung. Jabos overhead." The pilot of the lead Spitfire had seen the column and had correctly identified it as being German. He waggled his aircraft's wings as a signal to the rest of his squadron and put the machine into a steep dive in the direction of the bridge and the road on which 1st Battalion's column was now halted and under cover of the trees. The brief sibilant hiss of the Spitfire's rockets ended in crashing explosions as the projectiles detonated. Peering anxiously through the smoke Meyer was relieved to see that the bridge still stood. Now's your chance, he told himself. A second Spitfire will take about ten seconds to reach the same position from which the first had made his attack. You've got ten seconds, he told himself, to cross the bridge and reach the cover of the trees on its far side.

He pushed his foot down hard onto the accelerator and the Horch leaped forward like a stallion gored by its rider's spurs. Panzermeyer's eyes flicked from the road to the sky - no Spitfire had yet appeared. He would make it in plenty of time. But he had not fought the Western allies with their overwhelming air superiority and did not know of the old RAF tactic. An attack from ahead to hold the enemy's attention and then a second strike by an aircraft swooping in from the rear. The Standartenführer driving at top speed along the open road suddenly became aware of a furious whistling sound behind him, a sound which drowned out even the roar of the Horch's engine. That whistle vanished in the crashing detonation of two explosions. The first of these, striking on the right side of the road, canted the heavy vehicle onto its left wheels and threatened to overturn it. Then the second rocket exploded on the left side of the road and so close to the left side of the car that the heavy vehicle ended up in a ditch. Furious with himself for making such a stupid error Panzermeyer scrambled out of the vehicle, reached the road and began to shout at the Spitfires in coarse soldiers' language.

One after the other the fighter-bombers dived and fired. Their intention was clear. Destroy the bridge and the German column was immobilised, unable to advance and only able to turn round with difficulty; while the vehicles were manoeuvring they could be attacked at will. The RAF pilots were fully aware what their attacks would achieve and so was Panzermeyer. As if reading the enemy pilots' minds he knew that the trapped column had to fight back. He also knew that he had to demonstrate to his men contempt for the allied attacks.

"Vicious bastards," he roared out again, standing in the middle of the narrow road and shaking his fist as the Spitfires roared low firing their onboard machine guns. He knew that his demonstration would give the lads a bit of a boost. Tonight they would all be talking amongst themselves and asking, "Did you see the old man standing there. By God, but I thought he'd have a stroke. Didn't care a damn for the Jabos or their rockets…" Yes, it was a good demonstration. For a short time he continued to stand in the open and then he turned round and began to issue orders.

"Get the 20mm flak into action. Let's make it as hot as we can for the Tommies. "

Within seconds the small-calibre anti-aircraft guns were firing. It was little more than another demonstration. It was unlikely that the gunners would hit anything, but he knew the sound of the column firing back would calm rattled nerves. Perhaps it was the barrage which the 20mm guns put up or perhaps it was that the RAF squadron had run out of ammunition; but with one final shoot-up the planes flew away. "Cease fire" and there was a sudden deep silence. Panzermeyer swung himself onto the running board of a half-track and looked back along the length of the column. There were no fires and there seemed to be no damaged trucks. He whirled his hand in the air, the hand signal for the drivers to start their vehicle engines and seconds later waved the column forward. The vehicles crossed the bridge in a nose-to-tail column, picked up speed and began to make good time. Then at a cross-roads the head of the column ran into a press of vehicles. A large, unwieldy traffic jam had built up which sweating officers and bellowing NCOs were doing their best to clear. Meyer dropped from the running board and approached a young Army officer who was trying to regulate the press of road traffic.

"What's wrong here? Haven't this lot any movement schedules?"

"Certainly,- Standartenführer. But they are useless" and the Lieutenant held out a sheaf of documents. Meyer read them quickly.

"Stupid sods," he barked. The staff officers had worked out time tables based on vehicle columns driving at speeds applicable to a daytime exercise under optimum conditions. Under those ideal circumstances the timetables might have been kept. But as a result of Panzer Group West's conflicting directives the roads allocated for the movement of 12th SS had not only been reduced in number but those which remained had been allotted to other formations. Those facts and the delays caused by the allied Jabo attacks, had turned the carefully-timed movements into a nonsense.

"Right. I'll keep my column on this road and under cover," Panzermeyer told the Lieutenant. "Keep that panzer column in position there," he pointed to another tree-covered lane, and then pointing to a third road, "and that one over there, keep it under the trees. Let the recce units through, then the Panzer companies, then my 2nd Battalion. Finally, my 1st Battalion column will move, although it is clear we'll be stuck here until last light." He looked up at the sky. There were a few more hours of daylight and danger before night closed in and brought an end to the allied aircraft attacking the vehicle columns.

"Tell the men in the halted columns to get away from the vehicles and into the fields..."

"Even the drivers, Standartenführer?," asked the Army lieutenant.

"Certainly . We don't want them killed in their cabs if the Jabos make a successful strike. Everybody out into the fields. Well spread out, under bushes if possible."

"Shall I tell the men to fire their small arms against the Jabos?"

"There isn't much point. They won't hit anything and it'll only draw the Tommies' attention to them."

"It's pretty rotten having to squat down under fire and do nothing, Standartenführer."

"You don't have to tell me that, lad, I know it is but tell the lads to eat their haversack rations. It won't be much - bread and sausage, I suppose, but it'll help to pass the time. As for myself, I can do nothing until you come to tell me that my column can march. Not being able to do anything positive to help the situation, I shall find a leafy bush and have a couple of hours sleep. Wake me when it is time for this column to move."

The young lieutenant saluted and hurried back to the traffic jam at the cross-roads.

As a result of contradictory orders and delays only fragments of Panzermeyer's Regiment reached Caen during the evening of 6th June. The 1st Battalion reached Missy some 15kms south-west of Caen long after last light and dug in. Of the other two battalions of the Regiment and of the Regimental HQ, there was no sign. Late in the night of 6th/7th June, the scattered detachments of his regiment began to filter into the city, but 26th Panzergrenadier Regiment, the 1st Panzer Battalion, the mass of the Artillery Regiment and the Divisional train were a long way away. Having reached the first concentration area around Bernay-Lisieux-Vimoutiers and been ordered to move to a new area, the units were now trying unsuccessfully to force a way through the jam of military traffic which choked all the roads leading to the invasion area.

Allied radio interference grew throughout D Day and reached a peak by last light. The Allies knew very well that the evening hours were those during which there was maximum German wireless traffic. It was the time that headquarters chose to pass orders to subordinate formations and it was, therefore, from the allied point of view the best time of the day to carry out disturbance and interference techniques. That interference was responsible for the fact that a fresh order from Supreme Commander West to the 'Hitler Youth' was not picked up by every divisional formation. One unit which did receive it was the 1st Battalion of the 25th Regiment. Panzermeyer was with that unit.

The signaller clicked to attention as he stood on the rim of the slit trench in which the Commanding Officer was resting.

"Standartenführer, we are ordered to drive through Caen and to move into the area on the coast which is presently held by 711th Division. Action upon this order is immediate."

Panzermeyer knew his lads were worn out. The long hours of driving and the almost incessant air attacks had exhausted them. They needed sleep; so did he, for that matter, but obedient to the orders he had been given, he directed that the tired men be woken up and assembled. Half an hour later he was leading his 1st Battalion back towards Caen. The city had suffered a second massive air bombardment. If the scene after the first one had been apocalyptic the result of the second had produced a lunar landscape of huge stinking craters and piled up rubble.

"Runners!!!" and when they reached him Panzermeyer began to issue orders.

"You," pointing to one young lad. "Tell the Pioneer section to blaze a trail by putting up signs with our regimental insignia. You," to another runner. "My compliments to No 1 Company Commander. He is to put out picquets on the western exits from the town. Any of our regiment passing through are to be told that regimental HQ is at the Abbey at Ardenne, here..." and he pointed it out on the map. The young soldier nodded, but Panzermeyer still went through the military ritual, "Now repeat what I have just told you to do. The young SS man finished with, "...units are to group there at the Abbey at Ardenne." Satisfied with the report Panzermeyer ordered, "Right, away you go."

The Standartenführer thought deeply for some time. It was clear that it would take hours for the fragments of his Regiment to make their way through Caen's ruined streets and then across country to the Abbey at Ardenne. He needed to hold a battlefield conference, an O Group, but it was important that he let the regimental commanders know where and when this would take place. He rubbed his forehead in an annoyed concentration and then came to a decision. He would break wireless silence. Despite the Allied jamming some units would receive the message and act upon the orders he would issue. Those units would pass the orders on to any formations which had not picked them up.

"Signaller. Send to all units. An O Group will be held at 0200hrs in" he pause to recall the names of the cafe and the suburb. "...In the Cafe Verdun in St Germain la Blanche Herbe. All officers are to report."

It was long past midnight and Michael Wittmann had spent the best part of a day riding between the several concentration areas. It was late and he was both tired and hungry. While he was at Evrecy he had seen the second air attack upon Caen and had observed it with detached, professional interest. When it had finished he rode back into the city and, in the southern suburbs, found the Pioneers of 25th Regiment busily engaged in setting up posts bearing a shield with the unit insignia and number.

"Isn't that the tactical sign of the Hitler Youth?"

"Yes, Obersturmführer. We are the 25th SS Panzergrenadier Regiment."

"Ah, the very unit I have come to find. Where is the Regiment now?"

"Regimental headquarters is at the Ardenne Abbey; shall I show you on the map, Obersturmführer?"

"Yes, please."

"...and there is to be an O group at 0200hrs in the Café Verdun in the suburb of St Germain la Blanche Herbe - here, Obersturmführer..."

"Thank you, I'm very grateful." Wittmann mounted his motorcycle and set out through the ruins of Caen towards the small, intimate café where, in happier times, the young men of nearby Caen had brought their girls for ices and for citron pressés.

In the largest bar in the cafe, the SS officers of 25th SS Panzergrenadier Regiment gathered round their commander.

"Everybody here?"

Panzermeyer looked round the fresh, unlined faces of his subalterns. These lads of his were about to undergo their baptism of fire and from their faces it was clearly an initiation they were anticipating with pleasure.

"Right. Pay attention. The latest message received says that Division has orders to attack today, 7th June. But it is clear from other messages that no one else from our Division has reached this area and only this regiment is in position. So…" He exhaled in a long sigh, "It will fall to us to start the Divisional assault by ourselves. H Hour for our attack is 1600hrs. Intention: To drive the Tommies back into the sea…We did it at Dunkirk and in Greece, so you can say we have some experience in what we have to do."

Again he looked round the circle of faces. God, how young they are, he thought.

"All three battalions of our Regiment will be committed to the attack. The 1st and 2nd Battalions to form the assault wave, 3rd will form the reserve. Clear?"

He noted the nodding heads and then went on to detail objectives and boundaries. At length he stopped talking.

"Any questions?"

"The panzer support which you mentioned, Standartenführer. Will that be the Corps Tiger Battalion?"

"Not this time. It will be one of our own Panzer battalions. But Division has told me that the Tiger Company of Obersturmführer Wittmann is moving up and will support us in later battles. What…?"

"Beg to report, Standartenführer, I am here." Wittmann had joined the conference unannounced.

"Don't tell me you've brought your Tiger Company with you."

"No. I am alone…Just me. I came to see the situation on the ground for myself. See how the Tommies fight. A sort of pre-battle recce."

"Good man. Come back to my HQ with me when the O Group breaks up and we are finished here."

Panzermeyer looked, once again, at the young men in the room and realised that within hours some of them would be dead or mutilated. Quickly he dismissed the morbid thought. We are all soldiers, he told himself, and death is the soldier's constant companion. But again the thought intruded: They are so young. He began to speak softly, in an undertone, almost to himself.

"What our young lads do today, out there, will show whether or not we trained them properly to our own standards, the standards of the Leibstandarte. If we didn't, then a lot of them will be killed and it will be because of our failure…"

However softly the commander's murmured words had been spoken they had been overheard.

"They won't fail, Standartenführer," the firm, determined voice of Hubatsch, a Bohemian farmer turned soldier, radiated confidence.

Panzermeyer pulled himself together and reflected the enthusiasm of his subordinate.

"Of course, of course, Hubatsch. I am as sure of the lads as I am of anything. It was just a passing thought, that's all. Right, gentlemen" he addressed the O Group again. "To your posts. Sieg Heil. Ah, Wittmann, come with me please."

Chapter 6

The dawn of Wednesday, 7th June, was a glory of crimson and gold. From a tower on the roof of the Ardenne Abbey the battlefield on which Panzermeyer's 25th Panzergrenadier Regiment was to fight that day was laid out like a briefing model. Half right, that is to the north-west, were the villages, which were the objectives of his battalions. Farther away, behind those villages and some 16kms distant, lost in the blue haze of the horizon, was the Channel coast and the Orne river. An occasional, far distant sparkle, caught the eye as the sun's rays reflected from one of the swarm of barrage balloons which hung over the invasion fleet and the landing beaches. From the abbey roof and facing half left, that is to the south-west, clouds of smoke showed where the Tommies were laying down a barrage around Carpiquet. Directly in front of the abbey the undulating green of the Normandy bocage rolled down towards the Caen-Bayeux road, enclosing orchards, corn fields and small patches of woodland.

"Lovely view, eh, Wittmann?," and without waiting for an answer Panzermeyer went on, "Your Tiger Company will be coming under my command at some time. What I expect - no - what I demand is the closest possible support from you for my Grenadiers. Do you understand?"

"Perfectly, Standartenführer. It goes without saying."

"Well," grunted the Regimental Commander. "Just you see that you give it and my lads get it. We've got a hell of a task before us. I saw the allied invasion fleet yesterday. There are thousands of ships. If the Allies have that many boats just think how many tanks they will be able to put in against us. That's why I need the very best support you can give."

"I repeat, Standartenführer. It goes without saying." Wittmann was annoyed at the senior officer's attitude. It implied that he and his comrades would abandon the Grenadiers and leave them in the lurch. Panzermeyer noted the stiffness in his subordinate's voice and in an effort to conciliate the touchy subaltern asked him,

"What's your total to date?," referring to the number of tank kills that Wittmann had achieved on the Russian Front.

"I don't know exactly. A hundred and ten confirmed, I think."

Wittmann's war had been a very successful one so far. From the time that he had been given command of his first panzer in Russia he had scored victory after victory. Once, in a single day's fighting he had knocked out twenty-five of the enemy - eighteen tanks and seven SP guns. Anti-tank guns he had not bothered to include in his 'bag', although on that day he had destroyed twenty. Wittmann was a countryman with an instinctive eye for ground, like most men raised in the country and he was a patient hunter. Such a combination of skills, when translated to warfare and particularly to armoured warfare, had brought him a string of victories over his enemies. Now, in North West Europe, he was up against fresh foes with unknown types of tanks and new tactics. If the enemy was as numerous as Panzermeyer had said they were, then he would need all the skills that he had gained on the Eastern Front and more besides.

"Come, Wittmann. No offence was intended, either to you or to your men. Come on, let's go in to breakfast."

After the meal the two men sat silent in the abbey garden. There were questions that Wittmann needed to ask. He was too much of an introvert to phrase them bluntly but he knew that if he and Panzermeyer sat there long enough then the time would come when he could express what was in his mind.

The Regimental Commander waited for Wittmann to express his thoughts. He himself was in no hurry now. His orders had been issued and there was little he could do but to rest himself and to prepare mentally for the strain of command decisions that would soon come pouring in. There was a long, long silence. Then Wittmann, feeling that the time was right, spoke out.

"Standartenführer. If the Amis and the Tommies have so many tanks how will we be able to halt them here in France? The great mass of our own Army is in the East"

"Simple," responded Panzermeyer. "Remember your history lessons? Do you recall how the German Army held the Western Front for four long years by manning a trench line in Flanders? The same situation obtains here in Normandy, only here the bocage will be our trench line. It's a sort of jungle. All we have to do is to fight a jungle type campaign here in the bocage against the allied armour. That way we'll stop them. Time is on our side, Wittmann, not on theirs. The Führer has produced secret weapons.

Once they are in operation we'll crush the Anglo-Saxon bastards. All we have to do is hold here - here in the bocage until the Führer's weapons go in...and that, I assure you, will be very soon now."

Although he had never experienced it, Wittmann reflected on what he had been told about the bocage. It was, according to report, a lush, green countryside which ran inland from the coast, thick and impenetrable until it met the more open land south of Falaise. That bocage area was a mass of hedges, so tall and so thick that vehicles could not leave the road which ran between them, nor force a way though them, but were hemmed in, imprisoned between the cool, green lanes. In the bocage the defender had all the advantages. Wittmann considered that terrain factor. With luck and with skill the German Army in Normandy could hold out as the trench lines in Flanders had once held out. All that was needed was to keep a grip on the soil of Normandy until the Führer's secret weapons brought the Western Allies to the armistice table begging for peace. It really depended upon the calibre of the men who had to hold the ground

"Your Grenadiers…?" The question was impertinent and it died on his lips, but Panzermeyer realised what Wittmann was asking.

"The rank and file are green, I'll grant you that. They've not been in action yet, of course, but they're as keen as mustard. They'll be first class soldiers once they've been shot over a couple of times and have learned the score. Their average age is 18, but the senior NCOs and officers are all like you; veterans of the Eastern Front. We've trained our Grenadiers to be warriors; not with bullshit parades or learning how to goose-step like Frederick the Great's Grenadiers. We trained them with live ammo; shells and bullets. Six per cent casualty rate until the lads learned the lessons. On the last exercise, our fall-out rate was one per cent and most of those casualties were not gunshot wounds but broken limbs from falling out of trees. I'll give you, the lads are green, but they're good.

"Such confidence, Standartenführer. Such confidence in green troops!!!"

"And with good cause, Wittmann. My lads…do you know they're too young to qualify for a cigarette issue or for a ticket for a brothel…we give them sweets instead of cigarettes. Anyway, they've developed a tank-hunting technique that they are just aching to try out on the Tommies. It's close-quarter stuff, putting charges by hand on the outside of the tanks. Here in the bocage with that sort of trick they'll crucify the allied armour. I tell you, each Grenadier is a warrior and we've got nearly twenty thousand of them in this Division. They won't let you down. Just you see that you live up to their quality. Savvy? Right then, let's go up on the roof and see my boys get ready for their baptism of fire."

Chapter 7

It was not usual for the senior officers on the staff of Field Marshal von Rundstedt to be present at evening briefings. Those officers who did attend were usually aides de camp or adjutants who then reported back to their superiors the salient points of the day's events. The briefing for 12th June was, therefore, unusual in the number of very prominent commanders who gathered in what had once been the grande salon of the château which now housed the Field Marshal's H Q. The reason for the presence of so many senior officers was the critical situation in the invasion area and they hoped to hear of the measures that were being taken to meet the allied assault.

Colonel Burkdorff, duty officer of the day, stood with his back to the large wall maps holding a pointer in his hand. Quickly he disposed of the routine directives from OKW and then went on to the situation reports which had come in from the armies in the field. The sitrep for which the officers were waiting was that from Dollmann's 7th Army; the one fighting to contain the allied perimeters.

"Seventh Army reported that Carentan fell today." The Colonel's well modulated voice echoed round the salon. "This means that the American beachheads have linked, here and here ," he pointed with his stick to the relevant areas. "Our forces did not have the strength to prevent this." He sipped water from a glass and continued, "Seventh Army's sitrep advised that 1st SS Panzer Corps will hold its present position but will thin out its front line units in order to build up a counter-attack reserve. You will note here," he turned again to point to the map N…that a dangerous gap exists on Seventh Army's left flank between Panzer Lehr Division and the 352nd Infantry Division. This is a critical situation and one which the Anglo-Americans will surely exploit, even though their operations to date have been described as just weak probes. The Supreme Commander West has ordered, accordingly, that the gap be closed using all available resources. The forces immediately available to be committed are the recce battalions from the 2nd Panzer Division, from Panzer Lehr Division and from 3rd Fallschirmjäger Division. The 2nd SS Panzer Division 'Das Reich' has also been ordered forward and the first wheeled units of that formation will be put into the line as they arrive on the battlefield…"

~

On the other side of the Normandy battlefield British and

Canadian commanders were aware that although their attacks against the German positions to the south-west of Caen had produced no real breakthrough they had succeeded in forcing apart the Panzer Lehr and the 352nd German Divisions. If allied armoured units could exploit the gap which had been created between those two formations and could move swiftly enough then Villers-Bocage and the strategically important high ground around that place could be taken in a coup de main. A success on that sector would outflank the German troops holding Caen and they would have to either give up the city or face the possibility of being surrounded. The Allies needed an elite armoured formation to carry out such a task and one was to hand; the Desert Rats, the 7th Armoured Division. General Erskine, its commander received his orders and created a strong battle group around 22nd Armoured Brigade. That battle group was directed to work its way between the two German formations and then to pass around the left flank of Panzer Lehr Division after which it was to drive with all possible speed for Villers-Bocage and the strategic high ground. X

7th ARMOUR SERVED IN N. AFRICA ALAMEIN – Sicily + ITALY

~

The commanders of both sides were aware of the dangerous situation on the left flank of Panzer Lehr. British 2nd Army had begun to move troops in an attempt to exploit that German weakness but at the level of 1st SS Panzer Corps, that open flank was not the Supreme Commander West's strategic emergency but a threat which had to be dealt with immediately. Lacking other troops which could be put into the breach, Kraemer, Corps Chief of Staff, brought out of reserve the Tigers of 101st SS Heavy Panzer Battalion and ordered the unit to hold the ground around Villers-Bocage. For a short period of time, for a few days in June 1944, the main efforts of two armies, one British and one German, were concentrated around that small market town.

~

On the day before the events which are described above took place Sturmbannführer von Westerhagen, the Commanding Officer of 101st SS Heavy Panzer Battalion, was seated outside the tent which was his TAC HQ. He looked up as a shadow fell across the message he was reading.

"Ah, Michael!" He rose to greet his subordinate.

"Obersturmführer Wittmann, reporting as ordered." The formal method of reporting was delivered in regulation clipped tones.

"Welcome back, Michael." The men shook hands. Von Westerhagen was in a good mood.

"Standartenführer Meyer has sent a glowing report on your part in the battle for Buron. Excellent work, but, well, that is in the past. The immediate concern is the gap on the left flank of Panzer Lehr. Are you in the picture?"

Wittmann shook his head. Quickly the commanding officer of the 101st gave him the details concluding with the news that the first elements of 2nd Panzer Division, the lorried units, were not expected to reach Villers-Bocage until 12th June at the earliest. "We have to hold the line until they come forward in strength. We shall move to the Villers-Bocage area tonight in order to cover that gap on the left flank. But you won't have heard of the trouble the battalion has had since the order came for us to move from Beauvais. "

Again Wittmann shook his head. "Well," von Westerhagen continued, "We lost most of No 3 Company and the Workshop Company in an air raid. Then there were no trains to transport us so we had to carry out a road march. Even the best efforts of our shit-hot maintenance crews could not prevent a lot of Tigers dropping out en route. Now we have been ordered to form a deep defence across a wide sector of the front and the unit is only at half strength."

Von Westerhagen was deeply conscious of the responsibility which was his. All that his Command could achieve would be to occupy high ground and hope to have time to concentrate its strength before the Tommies came into view. He had cause to be concerned. According to early Signals Branch intercepts of British wireless traffic, a major British formation was preparing an offensive to take out Villers-Bocage. More up to date and more detailed analysis of the wireless messages identified that unit as a Brigade of Montgomery's 7th Armoured Division. An entire British Armoured Brigade would soon be leading the desert veterans of 7th Armoured through the gap and to oppose that elite British formation there were only a small number of armoured cars and the remnants of 101st SS Heavy Tank Battalion. It was a situation deeply worrying for von Westerhagen.

"It's a real brute of a job we have to do, Michael," he concluded his briefing. "Now please rejoin your Company - it is in a small wood just to the south of Montbrocq, that's a small hamlet near Villers-Bocage. With luck we should receive at least four hours notice if anything happens, so this allows you to spend some of the day resting. From the tone of Panzermeyer's letter," he tapped the paper with his index finger, "you could do with a rest. My Kübelwagen will take you back to your Company. I tell you Michael, I am relieved that you are back with us again."

* DID THE ASSAULT ON JUNO BEACH

Chapter 8

When there was time to think about the landing in Normandy the Canadians of the attack wave realised that this had not been as bloody as they had feared it might be. There had not been those massive casualties during the run-in that had been forecast and by last light on 6th June, the 3rd Canadian Infantry Division and the 2nd Canadian Armoured Brigade had a firm hold on Juno beach. There had been, of course, the usual cock-ups, but the worst thing that the first wave had had to endure was the waiting to set out from the harbours of southern England. That and the God-awful trip penned below decks until the time came to leave the mother ship and to clamber down her sides into the landing craft.

It had been all very well for those bloody matelots to shout 'hurry up', but it hadn't been easy to scramble down the nets in full battle order and to drop into a boat that was jumping about like a bitch in heat. And once you were in the swaying, yawing, flat-bottomed bitch of a landing craft then there had been the run-in. The boat stank of vomit as one poor bastard after another hawked his ring and spewed his guts up. It had been bloody cold, too. The spray soaked everything and, to cap it all, thunderous crashes and explosions had tossed the assault craft about like a cork. Of course, Jolly Jack Tar had said that they were our Navy's guns going off, but whoever believed anything that a sailor said?

A belly-churning crunch. We've grounded. "All out ". We drop four feet into freezing cold water and wade through the surf. The beach, at last. The frightening thought - didn't they tell us back in the UK that all the beaches were mined? What had they told us? That the German 'S' mine blew up when you walked on it and scattered hundreds of ball bearings at waist height. That Schuh mines blew off your feet...whip, whip, whip...Christ, that was sniper fire and too bloody close for comfort.

Who is that clown up there on the beach yelling at us to move off inland?

Another bloody sailor, the Beach Master. There are no mines so he says...We move off. Just behind the beach we see our first dead Krauts. Near them are some prisoners. We look them over. They're poor types...Bloody hell. Three of them are Chinks or something and the whole lot are as bomb-happy as buggery.

The Company Commander's waved us to halt. Thank God for that. Now for a quick smoke and a look around. So this is France. Funny, it doesn't look very foreign. Anyway we've made it. We're ashore and alive so far.

There's the noise of tank engines from the beach. It's the 2nd Armoured Brigade moving out. One of their regiments, the Sherbrookes, will be supporting us. They're a cracker mob. We'll be all right with them. Our Corporal comes back from O Group and tells us that our objective for tomorrow, 7th June, is a place called Carpiquet. It's miles inland. We are to move out at first light.

~

For a long time the Canadian infantry and armour groups met little opposition to their advance. There were some isolated rifle shots and a few machine gun bursts. But then, just outside the little village of Buron, they were struck by shellfire from a single, inadequately camouflaged 88mm gun; the last survivor of an entire artillery regiment. The commander of that regiment, Major Groschke, was not an emotional man but he was close to tears when he thought about the fate of his little Command. It had been slaughtered and the battle was not two days old. The survivors of the regiment's 1st Battalion had been caught and destroyed by an allied barrage. Those few who remained from 1st Battalion had joined 2nd Battalion as it moved towards Buron. The regiment had been ordered to hold that village ground, but long before the guns could reach the village and unlimber, low-flying Typhoons had dived on the slow, horse-drawn columns as they moved along a bocage lane. A three minute rocket attack by the RAF destroyed a unit that had been three years in the making. Out of all the regiment's guns only one 88mm had not been smashed and now Groschke and the survivors of his unit were manning that gun determined to hold Buron as they had been ordered. Their stand might well be heroic but could only be a brief one. There were only 20 rounds of HE ammunition left. All the tank-killing armour piercing shells had been lost in the Typhoon attack. Columns of black smoke marked where the regiment's ammunition carts had blown up and were burning.

From the direction of the coast came the noise of tank engines. They were not likely to be panzers moving about in daylight so they must be allied vehicles. "Stand to. Here comes the enemy." Major Groschke lifted the binoculars to his eyes. He had worked out the range to a metre. "Fire" and the first shell whizzed across the sky to burst above the Sherbrooke's leading tank. Crack, crack, crack!!!! Three more air bursts. They were only a gesture. High explosive could not 'kill' a tank. A quick order over the Sherbrooke's radio and four Shermans swung their guns towards the single 88. The flash of the fifth shell from Groschke's gun was answered by four flashes as the Canucks opened fire. Some of the German gunners were killed outright, others collapsed, mortally wounded. The old rallying cry of German artillerymen, 'Man the guns', died on Groschke's lips as the Sherman's second salvo exploded above his head. Now only two men scrabbled on the grass; the last of the whole regiment. The third salvo killed them, too. On the white dirt road the Sherbrookes waited but there was no more fire from the 88. They then resumed their interrupted advance.

There were also German infantry in the village; a scratch group of men collected from the stragglers of several units in 716th Division. That remnant had been formed into a battle group. For arms they had only rifles and a few machine guns; nothing else. How could they hope to delay, let alone halt the Canadian armour? They couldn't and they didn't. The battle for Buron was one-sided, bloody and brief. By 1130hrs the Sherbrookes had passed through the village and the leading tanks were advancing towards Authie. Back in Buron patrols from B Company of the Highlanders began to round up the last surviving Krauts.

Chapter 9

Wittmann and Panzermeyer stood on the roof of the Abbey at Ardenne and from that vantage point looked over a countryside which shimmered in the June heat. Wittmann felt it was a false heat. He could sense bad weather coming and lost the train of his superior's words as his mind considered how a storm in the Channel might delay the flow of reinforcements to the beachhead...He caught Panzermeyer's final words.

"Ah, look. There they go".

The two men looked down from the high roof and saw, looking for all the world like toy soldiers, Grenadiers springing out of troop carriers and half-tracks. The figures first appeared vivid against the steel grey sides of the vehicles but then disappeared as the camouflage jackets blended in with the foliage of the trees and bushes in the park. There was the sound of tank engines warming up. Instinctively, Wittmann listened. The motors were running well...good maintenance. He nodded approval.

"Ah, the heavies..." and Wittmann noted the enthusiasm in Panzermeyer's voice. Quietly the junior officer studied the Regimental Commander. He looks like a Slav, thought Wittmann. The same round bullet head, the hooded eyes, the high set cheek bones. Maybe his family had been Slavs way back in the 13th century when the Teutonic knights were colonising the East. But he must be pure-blooded now, otherwise he wouldn't be in the SS, let alone be an officer. A signaller sprinting across the roof with a message interrupted Wittmann's train of thought. Panzermeyer read the words on the message slip, cursed, moved forward to the edge of the parapet and rested his elbows upon the stone surface and focused his binoculars.

"Shit, shit, shit." He swore again and again in a harsh voice.

"Standartenführer?"

"One of 2nd Battalion's patrols has reported in. Look over there, Wittmann. See that shell fire? That's Buron. The Tommies have reached that far already. This report is from one of the standing patrols I've had out since first light." Panzermeyer pushed back the peaked cap from his forehead and rubbed a hand backwards and forwards several times. It was a gesture of annoyance and concern.

"Witt, our divisional commander, told me yesterday that the 716th Division had been completely smashed. They should have defended the coastal sector but the Tommies walked right over them. Now there's nobody on our left flank; nothing but a bloody big gap in our battle line and the Tommies are driving straight through it." Again he rubbed his forehead with a knuckled fist. For a time he was silent, weighing up the options.

"Right." He had decided on a course of action. "I can't wait until 1600hrs as I had intended. The attack must go in very soon now. I'll take 3rd Battalion out of reserve and put it in to beef up 2nd Battalion's effort. The attack will need armour. If only we had your Tiger Company…Well, we do have Wünsche's panzers. Ah, talk of the devil." he concluded as the elegant Max Wünsche, commanding the divisional panzer regiment, stepped onto the abbey roof.

"Max, I need as many panzers as you can spare for my attack. Put simply, what I need to know is the strength of the enemy armour coming through Buron. The Tommies are probably making for Carpiquet airfield. We've got to stop them. Send out a vedette, will you, to check the road from Franqueville to Authie."

"Certainly, Standartenführer." Wünsche picked up the mouthpiece of the Command set and checked the maps in his case.

"Achtung, Achtung. To Officer Commanding No 5 Panzer Company. Send out a vedette…" and he reeled off the map co-ordinates. There was a short wait. Then through the speaker of the set crackled the voice of the panzer Company commander.

"As ordered. Five runners at instant readiness."

Wünsche gave the short order, "Panzer Marsch," and the three officers watched from the roof as the Mark IVs moved out across the ground, now disappearing as they passed over a low ridge, now lost completely to sight as they were swallowed up in a bocage road, now appearing again as they climbed a slope. The five panzers approached the narrow road which links the two villages and the watchers saw them swing right towards Franqueville.

~

Staff-Sergeant Robson, in the turret of the Stuart heading the Sherbrooke column, watched in fascination as a string of red and green dots flew towards him. Almost hypnotised by their flight, it was not until the very last moment that his brain registered the thought that these were tracer bullets. Those pretty coloured dots could kill. He ducked his head in time but even above the roar of the tank engine heard the vicious crack, crack as the bullets flew only inches above the turret. He waited a few seconds and then looked up through the turret ring. There seemed to be no more tracer flying overhead now.

Gingerly, the Staff-Sergeant stood up in the turret and looked around. One glance was enough. Jerry had four machine guns in action and from the way the fire was being co-ordinated at a point above the road it was clear the machine gunners were pinpointing the column, 'spotting' for the heavy artillery.

"Driver. Halt." The Stuart stopped. "Sunray," Robson reported, "I am south of Authie moving towards Franqueville. There is machine gun fire. Four guns. Probably fixed line. I think the column is being pinpointed.

"Thank you, Leader." The Squadron Commander was on the set responding to the NCO's call. "Hold your present position. Four chums will pass and check the axis of advance from you to the objective minus one."

Robson took his Stuart to the side of the road and ran it deep into the bocage hedge so that the four chums - Shermans - could pass him. It would be a tight squeeze. The road was a narrow country one just wide enough for a pair of horse-drawn carts but certainly not wide enough for heavy armoured vehicles. The Shermans would carry out a reconnaissance of Franqueville, the last village before the regiment moved onto its final objective of the day, Carpiquet.

Robson's warning words made the Sherman crews more than usually vigilant. The vehicles moved slowly uphill towards Franqueville, gained the crest and from it spotted movement on a side road ahead and to the left of them. Although the commanders had only glimpses of the machines running along the bocage-hedged road, identification was immediate...panzers. Mark IV's. It was Panzermeyer's vedette approaching. The Shermans stood side by side at the entrance to the village forming a gun line. Ahead was the enemy. In a matter of seconds it would death or glory.

~

On the Abbey roof the three SS commanders listened to the voices of the panzermen coming through the command set loud and clear and with little distortion.

"See anything?" one of the voices asked.

"That's Porsch, the patrol commander." Wünsche said quietly.

"Nothing". came a second voice. "How about you?"

"Nothing...wait. Achtung, Achtung. Sherman tanks in Franqueville."

~

From the Troop leader of the Sherbrooke patrol fire orders rapped out.

"Five enemy runners moving left to right. I'll take the lead tank. Jeremy, you take the second. Sergeant Hackett, the third in the line. John, you take the fourth. Then we all concentrate on the last one.

The Troop leader spoke to his own crew.

"Gunner. Target. Enemy Mark IV tank heading the column. Range 450. Armour piercing. Aim, aim. Right. A bit more right, more yet. Steady. On? Ready? Open fire." The Sherman rocked as the main armament was fired.

~

The sound of an explosion came clearly through the command set on the Abbey roof. Then voices again. High pitched now with excitement.

"Auinger's been hit. He's on fire..."

"Yes, I can see...Ah, the crew's bailing out to the right. They're safe."

The sound of a second explosion crashed through the loudspeaker.

"Klempt? Klempt?" No answer. Porsch's voice became almost querulous. "Klempt? Klempt?"

"Here, Untersturmführer...I've been hit. We're bailing out. No casualties."

"What the hell's happening?" Panzermeyer was furious. "What the hell is the matter with your men, Wünsche?" He was deadly formal now, he no longer used the friendly name Max.

"With the men? Nothing, Standartenführer" replied the panzer commander, equally as formal. His tone was cool and his voice was not even raised. "What has happened exactly I do not know, but it is my belief that the speed with which our panzers went into action was slower than the Tommies. The enemy has Shermans, you know. They have powered turrets. We have only old machines whose turrets have to be turned by hand. It is a serious disadvantage in a situation where every second counts."

Panzermeyer forced himself to remain calm. His mind formed a new plan of battle.

"Right. That settles it. I am accepting that the Tommies are advancing in strength. Our attack cannot be delayed any longer. Signaller. Send to 2nd Battalion. You are to move into action in ten minutes. A panzer battalion will support our grenadier regiment's attack. Intention. First objective.....to recapture Authie. Second objective…to retake Buron. Additional message. To 3rd Battalion Commander. Your unit is no longer in reserve. It will reinforce the attack by 2nd Battalion. Action immediate".

Within minutes there was movement down in the Abbey park. Whistles blew.

Voices barked orders. There was a roar of engines as the panzer motors were revved up.

"Signaller." Panzermeyer called. "Entry for the War Diary. A patrol of No 5 Panzer Company met the enemy at…put in the map references, will you. At 1420hrs, the 3rd Battalion of 25th Panzergrenadier Regiment was ordered to support 2nd Battalion's attack timed to begin at 1435hrs. A battalion of the divisional panzer regiment was ordered to support the attack. Objectives…well you just heard me say them…Put them in will you? Now, Wünsche. Let's see your men move.

Now that action was imminent, Panzermeyer was his old self again; no longer nervous or fretful. He looked and felt years younger.

"Now, Wittmann. Come with me. I must be with my lads for their first attack," and the two men clattered down the Abbey's stone stairs, climbed into the commanding officer's Kübelwagen and set off to where 2nd Battalion lay waiting to go into action.

Chapter 10

The four Shermans of the Sherbrooke Troop stood undamaged, at the entrance to Franqueville. Their crews, talking excitedly over the intercom, were jubilant at the ease with which they had gained their first 'kills'. The whole operation had gone like clockwork. It had been easier than on a scheme in the UK.

"Sunray?" The Troop commander was calling up the Squadron leader. "Sunray minor here. We have killed three out of five. All confirmed. All three panzers are on fire. The other two have turned back. Do we pursue them? Out."

"No, repeat, no, Sunray minor. Stay in position guarding the road. We must keep it open for when the other Squadrons pass through us and move down to the objective. By the way, can you see Carpiquet?"

"Clearly. There's no sign at all of the opposition. None - either in front or on either flank. The whole countryside seems to be deserted. Can't see any civvies about, either."

"Sunray here." The Sherbrooke colonel was on the air. "Well done, everybody. Those machine guns which Staff-Sergeant Robson reported are still firing on us. I had hoped to get our gunner chums to stonk the enemy posts, but I can't raise the gunners on the air. Now: to all Squadrons. I think this is as good a time as any to have tiffin. To all Sunray minors: Let your men eat their haversack rations and let them brew up. Don't let them wander about. The villages are out of bounds to all ranks. I don't want anybody going into an estaminet. Out."

Seated alongside the bocage hedges the Highland infantry and the tankmen of the Sherbrookes ate their midday meal. Some way distant from them, on a low ridge to the left and in front of the Canadians, but unseen by them, Panzermeyer's patrols from 2nd Battalion were watching and waiting. A tap of Sturmmann Feldbacher's boot brought him sliding slowly down from the crest of the ridge back to level ground.

"Are the Tommies still halted?"

Feldbacher nodded. "They're eating," he reported.

"Have they put out picquets?"

"No."

"Right. Send half your Section to that bushy-topped tree over there. The 7.62 Pak are there. Your men are to help tow them into position. While half your Section is helping with the guns you take the other half Section down towards the road with panzerfausts and panzerschrecks. Tell them to be careful. No firing until ordered. Understood?"

"Certainly, Scharführer."

Gently, carefully and silently the high velocity anti-tank guns were manhandled into position. Their menacing barrels did not project through the trees and bushes but remained concealed by foliage until the time came when they would be ordered to open fire. Then it would take only a few seconds to push the guns through the leaves and branches and bring them into action. Other teams of Grenadiers armed with anti-tank rocket launchers worked their way stealthily down the bocage hedges and spread out to take up positions along the length of the Sherbrooke column.

Both groups of soldiers waited in the oppressive midday heat. The SS Grenadiers waited for the order to open fire and the Canadians waited for the order to mount up and move on to Carpiquet. The Canucks were unaware either that they were the targets for the SS groups or that those groups were now very close at hand. At the tail of the Sherbrooke column the commanding officer had finally made wireless contact with the field artillery regiment whose batteries were still on the beaches. The Sherbrooke colonel was involved in a furious argument with the Gunner commander. The tank man demanded that the guns blast the German machine gun positions. The Gunner officer told him that his regiment was beyond the range of 25-pdr batteries. The targets which the Sherbrooke colonel had indicated could not be engaged; not even with supercharge. Not at the moment, anyway. The Gunner was sorry but there it was. The Mediums would be able to reach him, sure, but they had not yet come ashore. When they did the Sherbrookes would get all the support they needed, but not before then.

The highly efficient German wireless intercept service picked up that titbit of information and flashed it to Panzermeyer as he drove towards the battle. The Standartenführer read the message and realised its significance. The Canadian armoured regiment was a God-given gift to his 2nd Battalion. The Tommies were unsupported. They would have to fight without the back-up of their artillery. Joyfully, Panzermeyer barked into the mouthpiece of the command set.

"Achtung. To artillery commander supporting 2nd: You will open fire now. Target: Column of vehicles and men on the road between Authie and Franqueville. Out. To Commander 2nd Battalion: Attack when the barrage goes in. Driver, stop the car. Let's get out,

Wittmann."

The two officers stood by the side of the Kübelwagen, their bodies taut with concentration. There was far away behind them a series of popping sounds and immediately a swift whooshing overhead as of unseen express trains. The 88s had opened up. The first salvo landed among the vehicles in the centre of the column. Seconds later another salvo crashed down, then a third. By the time the third pattern of shells had exploded the Sherbrooke drivers were back in their vehicles. Some intended to reverse towards Authie, others proposed to go forward into Franqueville. All sought to escape the storm of shells that was crashing above them and the lethal, solid, armour piercing shot that whizzed around them as the Grenadier anti-tank guns opened up.

The platoons of Canadian infantry reacted immediately and went to ground, in the ditches which ran alongside the road. Runners dodging through the explosions ordered the Highlanders' 'C' Company to pull back to Authie on foot. The Bren gun carriers would join up with them there.

The air waves were a babel of noise as the Canadian tank men asked for orders. A voice, strong, decisive cut into the confusion.

"Sunray here." It was the commanding officer again. "All runners, pull back, I say again, pull back. RV in Authie. Out."

At the command the drivers revved up, gained maximum power and locked one of their tracks so that the vehicle spun on its axis. One after the other and under fire, the armoured machines turned and were soon facing up the road towards the little village of Authie in which they hoped to find cover from the German barrage. Before the first of them was able to move off Feldbacher's Scharführer tapped him on the shoulder. The order to fire had come through from battalion. The signal to go into action had been given at last. The two Grenadiers pushed their way through the high bocage hedge and jumped onto the road.

"Sergeant Rudling…Sergeant Rudling," the voice was high pitched with excitement. "There's a couple of Krauts on the road by the side of your tank. They're carrying some sort of long pipe, like a drain-pipe." The sudden inhalation of the speaker's voice came clearly through the ear sets.

"Christ. It's a weapon. They've fired the bloody thing. It's a rocket." There was the sound of rapid machine gun fire as the bow gunner opened up but the two SS men who had fired the panzerschreck were already back in the cover of the hedge. A soft whoofing sound from the road told the pair that the Sherman was on fire

"Bail out, bail out, Rudling." But nobody escaped. The Sherman, known to allied tankmen as 'The Tommy Cooker', had demonstrated once again its terrible reputation for incinerating its crews.

The vehicles in front of the 'dead' tank were uncertain what to do. They couldn't manoeuvre past Rudling's tank; the road was too narrow. Unwillingly, they asked for advice.

"Sunray, Sunray. Sergeant Rudling's bought it. His vehicle is blocking the road. We can't get past him to tip it over and we can't push it off the road."

"OK. Advance into Franqueville. Wait for us there. Out."

Once again the vehicles of the Sherbrookes, still smothered by the barrage of 88mm shells, turned round and began to move towards the village where the panzers of Wünsche's vedette were still burning.

"Funny. There should be three smoke columns," thought Staff-Sergeant Robson. But he could count seven. His Stuart was a long distance ahead of the other tanks as it climbed up the slight hill towards Franqueville. On the crown Robson saw that the four new fires were blazing Shermans. The Squadron's lead Troop had been destroyed. In the confusion of the sudden bombardment from the 88s the Troop had stayed in the village seeking shelter among its houses, but there had been no shelter. Instead the Shermans had been surprised by panzers of Wünsche's 5th and 6th Companies moving forward to support 2nd Grenadier Battalion. All four Sherbrooke machines had been destroyed in a single salvo before they could send a message.

"Driver. Halt." Robson was now horribly aware of danger. He could sense it. It was an almost tangible thing. His skin prickled with fear. Then he saw Death moving forward to take him in the form of a young German who had jumped onto the road and was racing towards his tank. The SS man ran alongside the machine, halted and then placed a hollow-charge mine on the Stuart's side armour. He pulled the detonating cord and rushed into the bocage hedge.

A thundering explosion rocked the Stuart. The engine died. Screams came from the driver's compartment. Dust hung in the air mingled with the acrid stench of explosives.

"Ted? Ted?" No reply. Robson's brain registered that the bow machine gunner was probably dead. "Charlie? Charlie?" But from the driver came only screams as he looked with shocked eyes at the fountain of blood that was erupting from the arteries in his shattered leg.

" Frank? Frank?"

"I'm OK, Sarge." Well, thank God the gun layer was all right.

"We'd better bail out and see if we can help Charlie. Right, let's go."

Shaking and half deafened from the detonation of the mine Robson climbed out of the turret, down the outside of the machine and stood on the road. Frank joined him there. They looked into the driver's hatch. The pumping fountain of blood was less violent now. The driver had nearly bled to death. There was nothing they could do for him; death was only a matter of time and he was already unconscious.

The young SS man came back through the bocage hedge and onto the road. "Hello Tommy," he shouted to them. The two Canadians turned to face him. He gestured with his machine pistol and they raised their hands in surrender. There was a broad smile on his face. He had just earned himself a commendation by knocking out this Ami tank and the war was only a day old and his part in it a matter of minutes. It had been a very easy victory. So easy. Much simpler than the training on the tank destruction course. He took his hand from the magazine and let the machine pistol dangle from his right shoulder. From a pocket he took out a notebook and pencil, checked the time by his wrist watch and then noted down the Stuart's military number.

"Amerikaner?" He asked.

Robson shook his head. "No. Canadian."

"Engländer?"

"Canadian," said Robson very slowly and very clearly.

The SS man noted down the regimental title patch on Robson's shoulder and checked it with that on Frank's uniform. Then he walked away but had not covered more than six paces when he turned as if he had forgotten something. Gripping the butt of his Schmeisser machine pistol he swung it upwards and gripped the magazine. Then in single long burst of fire he shot the two men. Prisoners were an encumbrance at this precise moment, now that some of the Shermans of the Sherbrookes were climbing uphill towards Franqueville.

The commander of the first Sherman could see that Robson's Stuart was halted but he had not witnessed its destruction. From his turret he could see no damage and tried to raise the Staff-Sergeant on the radio. Annoyed at the lack of response to his calls, he drove up close behind the halted tank and climbed out of his turret to investigate the mystery of Robson's silence. Behind him on the narrow road the other machines closed up. To the Germans this was an unbelievable piece of good luck. By tuning to the Sherbrooke radio frequency they had learned that the road into Authie was blocked by one blazing Sherman and they knew from the victorious Grenadier that the road into Franqueville was obstructed by Robson's machine. This meant that the remaining Canadian AFVs, standing on the road, were trapped between the two knocked-out tanks. Not only could the Canadian armour not move backwards or forwards but it could not deploy off the roads. The bocage hedges were impenetrable by armour. The tanks could not break through them to gain the open country. Halted on the road they were sitting targets. The 5th and 6th Panzer Companies moved along the reverse slope of the low ridge between Authie and Franqueville. On the reverse slope they were out of sight of the Canadians trapped on the road. The panzers halted and spread out. A pair of Mark IVs of No 5 Company crawled slowly up the slope and passed over the crest.

"Kraut tanks, Sunray!!!!" came the loud yell as the two machines rolled into view. Each panzer commandant selected a target, fired at it and reversed his vehicle back into safety before the Sherbrookes could swing their guns. The flat crack, crack of the panzer 75mm main armament had been lost in the general noise of battle but the results achieved by the German gunners were shockingly visible. Two Sherbrooke vehicles had already begun to burn. From a point some two hundred metres farther along the ridge a pair of Mark IVs from No 6 Company moved up to the crest. Two more explosions. Another Sherman brewed up.

"Sunray, here. I can see what's happening. The Boche are trying to disperse our fire. We must be faster off the mark than they. We've got the advantage. We are firing from the halt. They're firing while on the move. We can get them before they can get...Here they come again."

The Sherbrooke guns swung towards a new pair of panzers and fired as the sights came on. A tank battle blazed and died within minutes. At its end eight Shermans had been knocked out and four Mark IVs from No 5 Company were out of action. On 6th Panzer Company's sector of the ridge there were ten Sherbrookes smashed for a loss of five German machines.

The immediate effect of that first battle was that the Highlander Company in Authie had lost its protecting armour screen. It would be defenceless against any swift strike which 2nd Battalion made against it. Panzermeyer summed up the situation very quickly. He shouted into the command set.

"No 5 Panzer Company: Get into Authie. Tempo! Tempo!. No 9 Grenadier Company: Accompany on foot. Move." and then to Wittmann. "Come on. Get into the Kübelwagen."

The panzers and the grenadiers swept over the open fields across the ridge and downhill into the small village. 'C' Company of the Nova Scotia Highlanders had had no time to prepare a defence. The German wave swept over them and through the village. The Grenadiers halted but the panzers continued the advance, passing out of Authie and along the narrow, dusty road to Buron. There it soon became clear that the lie of the land favoured the defenders. The country was less close than it had been near Authie. The ground was flatter and there was less cover. The bocage hedges ended only a hundred metres or so outside the village and the German armoured vehicles stood out in the bright sunlight, clearly visible to the anti-tank gunners whose weapons now formed the main Canadian defence line.

"On." The gun layers' shouts told the Company commander that each of them had a panzer in the sight. At 1200 metres the enemy vehicles were only little square boxes crawling slowly across the green meadows. Slowly, or so it seemed, the Mark IVs advanced towards the gun line. At a thousand metres the 17-pdrs opened up. As if they had been struck by a giant fist four of the panzers stopped and began to burn. A fifth was hit below the turret as it turned away and presented its thinner side armour to the guns. Another panzer was hit and began to burn as an incendiary shell struck it. Smoke from the burning machines hung like sable candles in the still, warm June air.

The remaining Mark IVs made smoke and under its cover turned back to Authie where the Grenadiers had regrouped, were collecting prisoners and wiping out the last nests of Canadian resistance. In a house at the end of the village Panzermeyer's quickly convened O group went over the second stage of the attack. Through binoculars Panzermeyer could see Canadian infantry outside Buron digging in, preparing defensive positions. He would have to move quickly before they were able to put up much of a resistance.

"Signaller, give me the set." And then to his supporting units, "to Regimental Artillery Commander: Barrages on Buron and Gruchy, now. To the Heavy Weapons Company: Close up and open fire on Buron. It is the next objective. Soften it up."

Within minutes German artillery shells had begun to crash down. Under cover of the bombardment three Grenadier Companies and the remnants of the two Panzer companies swarmed out of Authie and swung across the open fields.

Panzermeyer and Wittmann rode into battle in the commander's Kübelwagen, keeping abreast of the first line of jog-trotting Grenadiers.

"Exciting, eh Wittmann?"

"I prefer my Tiger. I feel I can hit back with an 88mm gun."

Panzermeyer halted the car, jumped out and pointed. Ahead and only a few hundred metres distant newly turned earth showed where the Canadian infantry had dug in. The Standartenführer dropped like a stone and pressed himself close to the earth. Wittmann and the grenadiers followed his example.

"Signaller," Panzermeyer shouted to the man still listening in at the radio. "Tell the Heavy Weapons Company to fire on that trench line ahead of us."

Although Wittmann had served with the 19th Infantry Regiment he had never made an infantry attack during his active service life. He was surprised at how slow and how relatively quiet was the battlefield. In his Tiger there was constant noise and movement was fast. Here on the ground there seemed to be little happening and even when the machine guns and mortars of the Heavy Weapons detachments went into action the noise they made was lost in the open air and seemed somehow muted. "For all that," thought Wittmann, "I wouldn't want to be a Grenadier."

Panzermeyer suddenly stood up. He knew he was in full view of the Canadians but slowly he dusted himself down in a deliberate act of bravado.

"Come on, Wittmann," and then to the young men who had stood up with him and were now waiting for his signal. "Follow me, lads."

The single line of SS soldiers moved uphill towards where mortar bomb detonations were crashing down along the Canadian trench line. Then streams of tracer flew towards the German infantry as the Highlander Bren gunners, defying the mortar bombs exploding all around them, opened fire. Grenadiers began to fall. Wittmann sensed that the attack was losing pace. He turned and faced the Grenadiers.

"Do I, a panzer man, have to show the Hitler Youth how to attack? Charge, charge." And waving his machine pistol he led the Grenadiers up the last few yards and across the Canadian slit trenches. In one of these a wounded Highland lieutenant swung a Bren gun, firing an arc of tracer from right to left. Bullets from Wittmann's Schmeisser cut him down. The Grenadier charge poured across the trenches. Then they halted and stood, panting with the effort, gasping for breath.

Chapter 11

"Well done, Wittmann," Panzermeyer grunted his approval then turned to the Grenadiers standing close by. "Some of you - you lot there, round up the prisoners. They can carry the wounded back into Authie. The rest of you, you men here, join one of the Companies attacking Buron."

The Regimental Commander and Michael Wittmann stood among the dead men and the scattered equipment which littered the Highlanders' position. Panzermeyer was silent, 'reading' the battle from the sounds of machine gun fire, from the crash of tank guns, from the explosion of mortar bombs and by using that indefinable sixth sense which good commanders possess. He did not like what he was 'reading'. It worried him.

"It's not going well, Wittmann. My lads have not yet taken Buron. Let's go and ginger up the attack."

"Have you thought," asked Wittmann as the two men made their way downhill towards the country road, "that the Tommies had prepared the village for defence and it is that, having to smash the Tommy defence, which is causing your Grenadiers to take so long to capture it."

"No. I don't think that's the reason. We are supported by the panzers of 5th and 6th Company. They ought to have smashed a way through for my lads by this time. We can't sod about spending hours fighting for every hamlet. Our task is to push the Tommies back into the sea."

"With respect Standartenführer, I don't see how one grenadier regiment and a single panzer battalion can hope to achieve such a victory."

"It's not just us alone, Wittmann. The 21st Panzer is also making a drive to the coast. They're on our right flank."

"Then they must be making a silent attack. Have you heard any sound of them? We have seen no liaison officers; there've been no patrols making contact with us. It strikes me, Standartenführer, that the main burden of the Army's counterattack rests on your three battalions and one of Wünsche's panzer battalions."

They reached and began to walk down the Authie-Buron road. From the direction of Buron a motor cycle combination came racing towards them. Panzermeyer gestured to the driver. The machine skidded to a halt only a few feet from them. "Take us as far forward as you can," he ordered. The Sturmmann swung the heavy machine round. The two commanders climbed onto it. Swerving, bucking and bounding in and out of shell holes, the combination brought them to a small track on the outskirts of the village. Panzermeyer's instinct had been correct. The German attack had begun to flag in the defensive fire of the Canadian infantry. Panzermeyer could neither hear nor see any panzers with the forward platoons. It was clear that his Grenadiers were fighting for the place without armoured support. The storm of rifle and machine gun fire from the enemy infantry in the houses along the southern edge of the village showed that they were prepared to fight, and to fight hard to hold the place. From windows and doorways the Nova Scotia riflemen fired at the attacking Grenadiers. Wittmann, sheltering from the fire, watched and listened. The enemy defence was uncoordinated and the fire was too high. That may well have been his assessment based on a veteran's experience, but the bullets were too close for one young soldier. He flung himself down sobbing hysterically behind a fence, clutching an MG42 to his chest with his body shaking and trembling. Wittmann prodded him gently with the toe of his boot.

"You won't kill any Tommies lying down there," he began in a conversational tone. "Now," and his tone was sharper and commanding, "Get to your feet and I'll name the targets you are to fire at." The boy still shuddered but began to rise to his feet, shamefaced. He laid his machine gun on the fence and stood, pale but determined, awaiting orders. In a shaken voice he tried to explain.

"Sorry, Obersturmführer, but my No. 2, my best friend, was killed only minute or so ago and..."

"Don't apologise lad, it has happened to all of us at one time or another. Don't worry, I'll get you a new No 2 - Hey you" to a Sturmmann kneeling and firing his rifle as precisely and calmly as if he were on rifle range and not in the middle of a close quarter battle. "Here you - take over here as No 2" and then turning to the shaken No 1, indicated the first target. "Look there. That yellow house. Top window. Give it a short burst." Bullets crashed through the window panes and drove back the enemy riflemen who had been framed there. "New target," the Obersturmführer began. "The window below - quick, lad - fire," as he saw the muzzle of a Bren gun project through the shattered glass and point towards him. The gunner sprayed the target with bullets and Wittmann noted with satisfaction that the boy was steadier now. There was no doubt about it; to fire a weapon in action really did inspire courage in frightening situations. Wittmann's attention was diverted suddenly from the boy and the chattering

MG42 by a sibilant, whispering sound. "Incoming shit," he thought. "That's all we need."

The urgent whistling overhead which had diverted him indicated that at last the Canadian artillery had entered the battle. The speed with which the Canuck gunners fired was unbelievable. A hurricane of shells was falling beyond the last houses and on the open fields across which the Grenadiers had charged. With a veteran soldier's instinct Wittmann knew that this storm of shells was produced by very few guns. This was no mass barrage of artillery like those he had experienced on the Eastern Front, but exceptional gunnery by a handful of first class soldiers. "It's as if their bloody guns are belt fed," he cursed as again and again he was forced to duck for cover from shells exploding in Buron's narrow streets. The Highlanders' CO had ordered fire to be laid on the village, prepared to accept a certain number of casualties to his own men in the houses, if the Krauts in the open streets could be caught and killed by the shells.

On the fields to the south of Buron, just beyond where shells were crashing down, a Panzer Platoon waited, deployed in line abreast. Standing in the turret of his Panzer IV, the young SS commander made a hand signal and the line of vehicles began to move towards the inferno of fire. Through his binoculars the Untersturmführer saw enemy armour moving about in the narrow, village streets. He assessed the tactical situation as his Platoon raced forward and came to a speedy decision. He would not make a frontal assault upon Buron. Instead would pull his vehicles back, divide his command and carry out a pincer movement which would not only isolate the village but would also trap the enemy inside it. For him to fight a tank battle in those confined streets could lead to his entire Platoon being destroyed for no advantage.

Urgently he spoke into the microphone mouthpiece. "All drivers - pull back - pull back..." This was not a manoeuvre which could be carried out immediately and for some time the panzers stood halted in the fury of the explosions. A group of medical orderlies, burdened down with wounded men on stretchers, staggered through the smoke and dust of shell bursts towards the vehicles. An NCO sprang onto the rear deck of the first machine and shouted the question in the tank commander's ear, "Are you pulling back?" The panzerman nodded. "Right, then" the Gefreiter shouted, "We'll put our wounded onto your vehicles" and without waiting for assent waved to his men forward. The medical orderlies laid the wounded on the sides and rear decks of the tanks, then clambered aboard to hold the stretchers in position with their hands.

Panzermeyer had been expecting the armour to come forward in support of the Grenadier attack and was astounded to see wounded men being loaded onto the panzers and to see the vehicles reverse out of the maelstrom of shell fire. "Good God, what are they doing? Wittmann..." he called to the Obersturmführer, "come with me..." A motor cycle combination carried the two commanders across the fields in pursuit of the Panzer Platoon. To Meyer the crisis point in the battle had come. He knew that his Grenadiers were outnumbered and that there were enemy tanks in the area. The panzers must attack, if for no other reason than to let the Grenadiers know that they were not being abandoned. His anger with the Panzer Commander drove from the Standartenführer's mind all thoughts of personal danger as he swerved the motor cycle through the shell bursts and raced alongside and then past the retreating vehicles as they drove up the road to Authie. He skidded the combo to a halt, and leaped from it to stand straddle-legged in the middle of the narrow road with one hand raised imperiously. The column halted. Panzermeyer beckoned to the young SS Untersturmführer who clambered out of the turret, jumped to the ground and doubled smartly to where the Standartenführer stood glowering with anger. Panzermeyer was not a man to hold his temper in check. Without bothering to acknowledge his subordinate's salute he flung the question.

"Where the hell are you going? What do you mean by leaving the battlefield without orders?" he began, "do you need to refuel or get more ammunition?"

"No, we have enough - but with respect, Standartenführer, my assessment of the situation was: it was not tactically wise to enter the village..."

Panzermeyer interrupted him. "I repeat, where do you think you are going? Do you realise you've left my Grenadiers to fight without your support? My lads don't go into battle with four inches of armour plate around them. If they can face the shit, so can you." He took a deep breath in a vain attempt to calm himself.

The young Untersturmführer began to talk. "The wounded Standart..."

"The wounded? The wounded? Do you think I was born yesterday? In my book you are deserting the field. Five tanks to carry the wounded back. And are you taking the wounded back? Don't you know that we have ambulances for that? Now get back inside your bloody armour protection and lead your men in. Your task is to support my

Grenadiers. Savvy?"

The young commander scrambled up the vehicle sides, dropped out of sight into the turret and then reappeared like a jack in the box. He spoke urgently into the chest microphone. The panzer engines roared to full power, hard lock was applied to one track and the vehicles began to swing around so as to face Buron again. The medical Gefreiter realised almost too late what was happening. The panzers were going into an attack with the wounded still aboard them. He dropped off the vehicle on which he was riding, lifted the wounded man from the rear deck and laid him on the grass. The tracks of another machine, spinning on its track to swing into line all but ran over him and the stretcher over which he was bending.

Panzermeyer's demand for immediate action took the panzers straight into battle and did not give the medical orderlies time to take off all the wounded. Some of those, together with the medical orderlies attending them, were still on the panzers as they raced towards Buron.

"Stupid sod," Panzermeyer swore. "That was a stupid decision to make, eh Wittmann?"

"No, Standartenführer. I agree with him. There is enemy armour in the village and the streets are too narrow to allow our men to traverse their turrets. Our guns are too long for such narrow streets. If one of our men has to traverse either right or left, he must find a street crossing wide enough for him to turn the turret so as to bring the gun into action. And, of course, an enemy tank may be waiting in an ambush position down that street. No, Standartenführer, I agree with the Untersturmführer. He was obviously intending to carry out a pincer movement…the obvious move…good God…"

He stopped aghast. The Panzer IVs racing towards Buron had reached a small cross-roads at the entrance to the village where a vedette of Sherbrooke Stuarts lay in ambush. The young Untersturmführer's tank stopped dead as a salvo of solid shot struck it. Seconds later there was a soft whoofing sound as the machine caught fire and then a loud explosion which blew the turret off in a single piece. The heavy metal turret flew through the air and crashed down upon a small estaminet, collapsing its outside wall. Panzermeyer and Wittmann pressed themselves to the ground to avoid other flying fragments.

The Standartenführer put his cupped hands to Wittmann's ear and shouted "I spoke earlier today of the need to give my Grenadiers every support. You must understand the infantry don't always realise why the armour moves back. They think the panzers are retreating. Can you understand their fears?"

Wittmann nodded. This fight at a different level - as an infantryman - had given him a new insight. Thoughts began to flow through his mind. Ideas on tactics and logistics. Well, concentrating on things like that helped to take his mind off the fury of the battle that was raging all around. The Sherbrooke vedette pulled back into cover leaving the two surviving panzers to drive forward into the village where the Grenadiers were fighting from house to house, "mouseholing" their way forward. The tactic they used was simple but effective. Satchel charges blew a hole in an interior wall of a house and into the clouds of dust and smoke which obscured the gap Grenadiers lobbed stick grenades. Dull thuds as they exploded and then the SS men stormed through the breach machine-pistolling to death the Highland defenders.

It was a tactic that did not always succeed. The Canadians protected themselves behind the heavy furniture in the rooms and then, as the Grenadiers rushed through the gaps which they had blown in the walls, the fire of Tommy guns and Sten guns cut them down. In the shuttered darkness of French peasant houses men died or fell clutching gaping wounds, moaning in agony or calling for stretcher bearers. Outside those houses, in the streets of Buron there was noise, confusion and death. Sherbrooke tanks, either singly or in pairs, often the surviving 'runners' of Troops or Squadrons, crashed their ponderous way, machine gunning any and every movement they saw. Too many of the regiment's vehicles had been blown up at close range for the survivors to risk anything. The Canadian tank men had learned very quickly the tactics of the 'Hitler Youth' rocket men. A Grenadier, firing a panzerfaust or panzerschreck, could halt an advance by knocking out the lead tank. Then, as the rest of the column was held immobile and impotent, out of the houses would rush agile lads with hollow charge mines which they fitted coolly and calmly onto the outside of the Canadian armour. Small wonder, then, that when Sherbrookes saw any sort of movement; whether this was inside a house or on the open street, their reaction was to shoot first and identify afterwards.

The confusion of battle was as hard for the SS infantry and panzermen as for the Canucks. The loss of groups of Grenadiers to the house to house fighting weakened the impetus of the SS attack and this began to slow and then to halt at the last houses in the northern end of the village. Beyond these the Highlanders had dug in and were grouped around their last remaining anti-tank guns. Their position formed a sort of citadel, a fortress inside which the Nova Scotias would make their last stand.

The Hitler Youth had lost a great many officers in the attack and Panzermeyer only became truly aware of how many when he and Wittmann reached the northern end of the village. There they found one group under the command of junior NCOs who were uncertain and shaken but still determined to advance. Panzermeyer realised the group needed the leadership of a veteran soldier.

"Wittmann. I must go back and find a command set. We have to have reinforcements. Get a grip on these lads. Hold out here. I'll bring other groups forward." The Regimental Commander left, weaving his way through the explosions which rocked the narrow street. Wittmann mustered his new Command. Fifteen Grenadiers and three NCOs. It was not a large group.

"Any others of us about here?" he asked. "Any in the house across the road?"

"About twenty, Obersturmführer."

"Attract their attention, will you." Faces soon appeared at windows on the other side of the street. "Who's in charge?" Wittmann called to one face. A voice answered him.

"Scharführer Weg reporting, Obersturmführer."

"Bring your men over here, Scharführer" and within minutes Weg's group had reported in.

"Scharführer, as I see it the Tommies are not yet properly prepared. If we attack we can drive them back. I propose to charge the enemy position. How many machine guns do you have?"

"Six and about 2000 rounds per gun. We've some hand grenades and rifle grenades."

"Right. Most of your men have rifles and not machine pistols. Well, we shall give the Tommies a taste of cold steel. They won't stand up to that. Now, Scharführer, put a pair of machine guns in this house and another in that house yonder. Before we charge put down a short barrage of rifle grenades, then rake the Tommies' positions with machine gun fire. I'll talk to the men now."

Wittmann was no orator but rather a quiet, introspective man unused to expressing himself. Yet now he had to inspire these boys to make a bayonet charge against a numerically superior enemy occupying a prepared position.

"Now, lads, you may not believe this but the Tommies over there are more frightened of you than you are of them. We are going to drive them back out of their trenches. It won't be easy, but if any of you feels his courage failing, remember the Führer's words, 'German youth must be as hard as Krupp steel.' You are the Führer's own Division. You cannot fail him. I know you will not fail him. Now, fix bayonets. We'll rush round this house and by the time we have reached that track there, we should be in extended line and ready for the charge. Remember, the attack is for Germany and for our leader, Adolf Hitler. Sieg Heil."

He waved his arm. It was the signal for Weg to open fire. Seconds later, rifle grenades exploded among the Highlanders' trenches. Spandau fire swept over the 'citadel' and then from behind the house the Grenadiers erupted. They doubled forward and formed a single line, each man holding his rifle across the chest in the high port position. Ahead of them ran Wittmann, tall and lithe, his dark hair blowing as he ran. He was bareheaded; his cap had been lost in the first paces of the assault. Quickly, he glanced from left to right down the line. The lads were shoulder to shoulder now. None of them was wavering. They were all dead keen. Only 50 yards to go. No fire was coming from the enemy. The moment for the charge had come.

"Hitler Youth," he shouted over his shoulder, "for our Führer, Forward," and he heard behind him the answering cry, "Mein Führer, mein Führer." The line of German bayonets came down to waist level. The enemy trenches were now only feet away and, as the Grenadiers reached them, the Highlander defenders rose to their feet, took up the 'on guard' position and prepared to meet the SS in hand to hand combat. Then, in the fields of Normandy, in the middle of a highly technical war, two small groups of warriors fought in the way that warriors had fought since the dawn of Time - hand to hand, man against man. The Highlanders' line was soon overrun and men began to surrender, firstly only singly but then in groups. Behind Wittmann and his exultant group there was the sound of whistles. Thank God for that. Panzermeyer had returned, bringing with him a group of men he had collected en route. "Message for you, Wittmann. The rest of your Battalion is coming forward. You are to return immediately. Sorry to lose you - You would have made a damned good infantry leader. You take the combination - I'll carry on with the attack."

The two men shook hands. Without a backward glance Wittmann left the Buron battlefield to return to his Tiger Company.

Chapter 12

A night of disturbed sleep did not leave No 2 Company of 101st in any mood to appreciate the warm but misty morning of Sunday 13th June. So far as the men knew this was likely to be a very dodgy day indeed. They knew that they were covering the gap which yawned in the German battle line and that their task was to hold until the mass of 2nd Panzer Division reached the battlefield. So today could very well be another day of battle against heavy odds.

But they knew, at least, they were not alone now. Nine Tigers of Hauptsturmführer Möbius's No 1 Company had reached the area and their crews were resting in a wood about a mile away. That increase in strength was welcome but the fact which gave Wittmann most concern was that there were, as yet, no infantry units in the immediate area. Armour, he knew, could not hold ground indefinitely. Only infantry could do that. Armour was not as flexible and was less mobile in certain operational situations than infantry. In any case to use panzer to dominate terrain was a misuse of the armoured weapon; everybody knew that. The single crumb of comfort was the news that the first infantry battalions ought to have reached his area before midday. Then the Tigers of the 101st could be let loose to play havoc with the allied Shermans and Stuarts.

Wittmann sat on the turret ring of his Tiger enjoying the June morning. The sun had dispersed the dawn mist but the day was not so far advanced that his vision was distorted by the shimmering waves of mid-June heat. In the clear still air everything stood clear and distinct. Wittmann could relax for a while. He had disposed the vehicles of his Company tactically. Two Tigers faced towards the Odon river valley, but were hidden in a little wood. Another Tiger was positioned beneath some trees on a small track running parallel to the Villers-Bocage-Point 213 road and at a point from which it dominated the northern exit of the village. Wittmann's own panzer was on the crest of the hill. Seated on the turret ring he was drinking coffee when a light, flickering miles away down in the river valley, caught his eye.

"What do you make of that, Woll?" he asked his gunner. "There, that light down in the valley."

"The sun reflecting from a windscreen, Obersturmführer. Enemy recce vehicles followed by armour," replied the gunner after a long and careful study. Then checking the position of the flashes of light he went on. "It's coming up from Livry and heading straight for us..."

"Obersturmführer..." the wireless operator interrupted the

gunner's observations. "Message from Corps."

Wittmann nodded. "What does it say?" he asked.

"Message begins: Obersturmführer Wessel of No 1 Platoon, at present with Panzer Lehr Recce Battalion, reports from his position on the left flank of Panzer Lehr Division, the movement of a large column of allied armour towards Villers-Bocage. Corps therefore orders, with immediate effect that the two Companies of our Battalion are to go over to the state of immediate alert. Two Panzer Companies of 'Hitler Youth' Division - one Panther and the other Panzer IV, have been ordered forward to support us. This Company will take any action it considers appropriate. Message ends," he concluded.

"Thank you. Now, Woll. The situation, as I judge it, is that we shall have to wait for the enemy to make his move. There is nothing to be gained by our moving into Villers-Bocage without strong infantry support. That would be absolute suicide. So we wait to see what the Tommies will do. On past form they will move deliberately. They will occupy Villers-Bocage and then spend a couple of hours messing about preparing to make the next bound. That gives us time to get ourselves ready and then, in conjunction with the Hitler Youth panzer companies, to attack and to fling the enemy back out of the village"

Wittmann had, however, made a false appreciation of the British plan. On 12th June, High Command had ordered 22nd Armoured Brigade to move fast and to take the high ground of Point 213. The Brigadier, understandably worried about advancing into enemy-held territory without proper reconnaissance, had asked for time to carry this out and had been refused. Time was the vital element, he was told. He must bash on. This he had tried to do but the Brigade advance had been dogged with bad luck from the outset. The leading units had just moved off across the start line at 1600hrs, on the 12th, when they were met with the fire of a Pak front supported by infantry. The massed anti-tank guns of the PAK front had caused casualties among the armoured units and had flung the battle plan into confusion. It had taken four hours to beat down the opposition, by which time the light was going and the Brigadier decided that a night advance through enemy territory was too high a risk to take. The Brigade bivouacked in Livry and had restricted its activity that night to gaining touch with 1st US Infantry Division on its right flank.

At 0530hrs on the 13th, the advance had been resumed. The point unit for that day was 4th County of London Yeomanry with the recce vehicles of 8th King's Royal Irish Hussars protecting the left flank and with the 11th Hussars carrying out reconnaissance on either side of the thrust line. At a cross-roads in the river valley an O group was held to set out the order of units for the next bound - beyond Villers-Bocage to Point 213 - the area in which Wittmann and his Company were waiting.

The O group allotted to each unit of the Brigade a specific task. The 1/7th Queens Battalion was to enter Villers-Bocage and to hold all the exits except those to the west of the church. The 1st Battalion, Rifle Brigade was to take and secure all the other exits. The tanks of 5th RTR were to occupy the high ground to the south west of Villers-Bocage while 26th Anti-Tank Battery was to cover the gap between the CLY and the RTR. It was an excellent plan. Infantry would hold the village, while armour and anti-tank guns guarded the flank which was open to a possible thrust by Panzer Lehr Division. The Brigade with its left protected and its rear secured would send the CLY in a lightning thrust uphill to reach Point 213 where it would consolidate. With a British armoured brigade in strength behind the German lines, the Boche in Caen would be outflanked and compelled to pull out of the city. The O group broke up, the infantry embussed and the recce units on either side of the point regiment moved at a fast pace across the Odon river valley and climbed uphill towards Villers-Bocage.

"Sunray! Sunray! Point leader here. I am halted in the main square of the village. There are no, repeat, no Germans in the place. The locals say that there have seen none for several days. Over."

"Alec! Alec! Sunray here. Change of plan. 1 RB are not to stay in the village but are to go forward in personnel carriers, to the summit. You may need infantry protection when you get there. The 8th Hussars have reported seeing Boche recce vehicles in their sector. Repeat - 1st RB to move with point unit to 213. Understood? Out."

But no other British formation reported seeing German units. There was no sign of them. It was clear to the Brigade officers that the enemy line had been so deeply penetrated that the Boche was unable to put up any sort of cohesive opposition. The drive uphill to Point 213 should be a doddle. A new message crackled into the Point Leader's earphones.

"Alec! Alec! Sunray here. New plan. You are not to capture 213 after all. You and 1 RB will halt on the road between Villers-Bocage and the hill crest. Some of our tank regiment chums and the Surreys will pass through you and take over as point unit. They will advance on 213. Your B Squadron is to stay where it is on the Caumont road and await further orders. Out."

That decision decided the outcome of the battle. When the message was sent the CLY's A Squadron and the Rifle Brigade had already driven out of the village and were well up the hill nearing the objective. At a point less than 400 yards from the crest the column halted as ordered. An O group was called. The officers gathered round the Commander.

"Everybody here?" He asked. Heads nodded.

"Brigade says that part of 5 RTR will pass through us. It is obvious that the road is too bloody narrow to take two columns of armour side by side. We shall move in as close as possible to the hedge to make room for RTR to pass us. I want to make our column as short as possible, so we will close the vehicles tight up - nose to tail - and as I have said, as close into the hedge as we can get so that the Tank lads can pass us without too much difficulty. It'll be a squeeze, I know...What is it, Charlie?"

"Sir," one of the CLY officers broke in. "If we close up nose to tail and are wedged into the hedge, we shall not be able to deploy in the event of an enemy attack..."

"Charlie," the tone was that of a tired aunt talking to a tiresome child. "Have you seen any sign of Boche armour? Has there been any report of Boche armour in our sector? No? Then what have you got the wind up about?"

"It just seems unwise, Sir," in a timid voice. "We are, after all, in enemy territory. God knows what might be hidden in the woods up there..."

"Don't be feared, Charlie. What I am proposing is a short, simple operation. We close up the vehicles of our column. That'll take five, ten minutes at the most. RTR passes us, ready for action. Another ten minutes. Then, once they reach the summit we shake out again into battle formation, tactically disposed. OK Charlie? Does that satisfy you? Right, some of you go off now and organise the closing up of the column . Then come back here. O group remains intact because we have to discuss what happens to unit dispositions and boundaries after 5 RTR has taken Point 213."

Wittmann now stood on the turret of his Tiger and watched the British column with interest. The tanks, the armoured personnel carriers and the Bren gun carriers on the road below him represented an overwhelmingly strong attack force. Farther away, back in Villers-Bocage, he could make out the movement of other British troops and in the fields outside the town anti-tank guns were being brought into position. The British units on the road below him were backed by another strong force in the village. He was aware that his appreciation of the situation had been faulty: Tommy had not spent time planning his next move but had thrust forward boldly in an imaginative way. Now - the question was, how could the Tigers of his Company create the maximum damage to the enemy column? Then the Obersturmführer saw the British make a tactical blunder.

"Good God alive," he breathed as he saw that the enemy vehicles on the road were being brought close to each other. It was clear that those in the centre of the column would never be able to drive off until the tanks at the head and at the tail had moved. And if those at the head and tail were prevented from moving, then the whole column would be immobile. What he saw before him was the panzerman's dream - defenceless enemy vehicles, unaware of the danger which threatened them and incapable of offering opposition.

It was obvious what he had to do. Knock out the first and last vehicles in the British column and then go on to destroy the armour in between the two wrecks. The trapped vehicles could neither turn round on the road nor break through the bocage hedge nor could use their main armament. This was not panzer warfare - this was the slaughter of the innocents. He had no time to give orders. Any minute the situation might change. He must act immediately. He dropped into the turret and grabbed the microphone. "No 2 Company - Listen for my orders. Out." and then to his own driver, "Panzer Marsch." The 56 ton Tiger charged downhill toward the unsuspecting British column.

As his panzer rolled into battle Wittmann spoke to the crew and then to the rest of the Company. "Commander to crew. We're in for a mad five minutes. In front of us there is a sitting target of 25 plus enemy vehicles who can't hit back. What I want from you, Woll, is really shit-hot gunnery. Once the main armament has opened fire you, bow gunner, will spray the enemy column with machine gun fire. Right, lads, get ready. "The huge machine bucked and reared its way downhill. Hidden from sight by the thick bocage hedge, none in the British column saw Wittmann's Tiger moving down upon them, nor did they hear it. The noise of his approach was disguised by the sound of their own vehicles moving closer together.

"Mother Tiger to cubs. Cub Bodo, keep your present position on the path. You are to halt any attempt by the Tommies to get off the road on your side. Cub Caesar, you will do the same as Bodo if they try to break through on our side of the road. Cub Dora, stay in position on the crest of 213, in case the Tommies try to break through in that direction. Commander to No. 2 Company - good hunting. Here we go."

By this time the panzer had reached the last vehicle in the British column. "Gunner, all rounds to be solid shot, no HE. Targets, enemy vehicles on the road. Range 300 metres. Report when on."

Woll, seated in the layer's seat, watched his No 2 begin the firing procedure. The breech block clicked open. Cradled in No 2's arm was an armour-piercing shell which he shoved into the open breech and rammed home. The breech block rose automatically and locked. A small red lamp glowed, indicating that the huge 88mm gun was ready for action. Woll pressed his eye to the rubber mounting of the sights and saw images flick across the phosphorescent horizontal and vertical green lines as the turret traversed. Then, almost filling the sight, he saw a Stuart tank. "On," he called and took a deep breath. His hand hovered over the firing button. "All guns fire," and Wittmann, standing in the turret, felt the exhilaration of a warrior as the battle opened.

A cloud of sulphurous yellow smoke from the 88 was blown away as the Tiger plunged closer to the road. A bright white flash, a dull red fire and a cloud of black smoke rising in the air, showed that Wittmann's first victim of the day was alight. Woll pressed the button controlling the turret traversing gear and listened with half an ear to its smooth running sound. The breech block opened, flinging the first empty shell case into a canvas sack below the breech. Another round was loaded; the red light glowed. Woll saw the outline of another vehicle and pressed the firing button. A half-track was struck by the high velocity shell which passed through it killing and wounding the men of the Rifle Brigade, men who were sitting inside the vehicle smoking and chatting.

"Driver - hard lock to bring us parallel to the road. More, more yet, that's it," and then again the crushing blow of the explosion as the third shell flew to smash another tank. A fourth, then a fifth and a sixth were destroyed in the first minute. The British reacted. Officers of the Rifle Brigade brought their platoons into firing positions along the hedge.

Machine gun bullets could not harm the Tiger, now arrogantly destroying the British vehicles as it cruised along the column towards the summit of the hill. Back in Villers-Bocage the sounds of battle alerted the other units of 22nd Armoured Brigade. The Queens Battalion began preparing the village for defence and the HQ Squadron of the CLY drove out to take control of the battle being fought on the road to the crest. In the market square personnel carriers were driven into side streets to clear the area and on the Caumont road the vehicles of B Squadron were halted awaiting further orders. Just below the crest of Point 213 the tank commanders at the head of the British column were making frantic efforts to bring their vehicles out of the confusion all round them and to get them into action. Wittmann saw them and appreciated the threat which they might pose. He decided to switch targets.

"Woll. Ahead of us just below the crest. The vehicles there at the head of the column. Range 400 metres. Destroy them..." The traversing gear swung the 88 away from the AFVs in the centre of the column and menaced those at its head. "On" called the No 1 on the gun.

"Fire" and Woll's hand pressed the firing button.

A brilliant white ball of light streaked towards the crest of the hill and disappeared in the thick greenery of the bocage. "Missed," he thought but then a violent explosion flung sections of the leading Stuart into the air. Woll, looking through the sights, was held by the spectacle and did not move until he felt the No 2 touch him on the arm and nod at the glowing red lamp. The gun was loaded. The Tiger shook as the gun fired and again the white ball of AP shot flashed, vanished and then produced the oily black plume of a petrol fire.

"Woll. Resume firing on the vehicles lower down the column."

A series of explosions from the 88 produced fires as one after the other the armoured fighting vehicles of the point unit of 22nd Armoured Brigade were destroyed. The road to the crest of the hill was strewn with dead and wounded British soldiers and littered with the burning wrecks of twenty-five armoured fighting vehicles.

"Signal from No 1 Company, Obersturmführer. Infantry from 2nd Panzer Division have now reached our area and are being committed to battle."

"My compliments to Hauptsturmführer Möbius. The Panzergrenadiers can go in against the Tommies on the road. Our attack must have disorganised them quite a lot."

And still the main armament crashed out and still the bow machine gun sent lines of tracer bullets streaking into the men of the Rifle Brigade lining the hedge.

"Obersturmführer - Woll here. We are running low on AP shot."

"Thank you - Driver - fuel state?"

"Half a tank left, but it would be wise to top up."

"Bow gunner?"

"About 4000 rounds fired. We could do with some more."

"Thank you crew. Mother Tiger calling Cub Caesar: Carry on with the destruction. I am off to refuel and to take on fresh ammunition. Out."

Back at A echelon, the fuel and ammunition distribution point, the excited talk was of the victory that Wittmann had won. More than twenty enemy vehicles were on fire; five others were immobile but were probably knocked out. Modestly, Wittmann brushed the praise aside.

"I've got a first class crew. It's not just me."

"But today's score is better than anything you achieved on the Eastern Front, Obersturmführer."

"Just say that I was lucky to be up against fairly green troops."

As soon as the armour-piercing shells were fitted into the racks, the fuel tanks filled and machine gun belts laid in place, it was time to return to the battle.

"Driver. Return along the same track until you can turn onto the main road. Now that we have the Tommies confused I'll risk a recce of Villers-Bocage." Then speaking to the other crews of his Company, "I am going into the village. Move from your present positions and follow me as quickly as you can. We can leave the task of wiping out the opposition to No 1 Company."

His Tiger lumbered downhill, not charging into action this time but rolling along in the fuel-conserving fifth gear. Wittmann studied the ground ahead very carefully, interpreting the sights and sounds that came to him. He looked towards the village but could see no movement there. It looked deserted.

"Driver. Get onto the road now" and the giant vehicle crashed through a flimsy wooden gate at the end of the path to turn onto the N175 just below the tail of the smashed British column. The road ran steeply downhill into Villers-Bocage. At the exit to the village Wittmann identified four stationary Cromwells; the vehicles of the CLY's Headquarters Squadron.

"Woll. New targets. 11 o'clock. Group of tanks on the east side of the main road. Do you see them?"

Woll, looking through the gun sight, rotated the handle of the sight drum. The No 2 switched on the electric motor and the turret began to swing round to the 11 o'clock position. "On" Woll called out.

"Panzer: stop." The Tiger halted. Wittmann rapped out the order. "Fire." The recoil of the explosions shook the vehicle. The leading Cromwell, that of the regiment's Commanding Officer, reeled under the impact of the solid shot which struck it and destroyed it. Immediately behind the CO's tank was that of the Regimental Sergeant-Major and in the third machine the Intelligence officer. Two shots from the 88 'killed' both their vehicles. Taking advantage of the confusion and covered by the smoke of the burning Cromwells, Captain Lee, in the fourth tank, ordered his driver to reverse it into a side street.

Conscious of the danger in which he was putting himself, Wittmann drove his Tiger slowly into Villers-Bocage. Ahead he thought he could see movement but could not immediately identify it. With his attention taken up with squinting through the oily smoke of the burning Cromwells, Wittmann had not noticed that Captain Lee's Cromwell had escaped and was hiding in the side street.

Richard Fairclough, commanding B Squadron of the CLY, waiting with the tanks of his Squadron on the Caumont road at the entrance to Villers-Bocage, was unaware of what had happened to A Squadron and Regimental Headquarters. It was clear that something had gone drastically wrong; there was no acknowledgement of messages sent to HQ or to A Squadron nor were any reports coming in from those units. But Fairclough could see, rising above the roofs of the low peasant houses, columns of smoke and he could hear the crash of gunfire coming closer. Despite the orders he had been given, to wait on the outskirts of the village, he decided to bring his four tanks to participate in a tank battle which, if he was any judge, was being fought on the far side of the village.

"Sunray here. We shall drive from our present position and go through the village. From now on we must expect trouble. All guns will load with AP. Sunray minors must be extra vigilant. Once through the village, we shall halt at the foot of the hill where the Caen road begins - see it? it's marked N175 on your maps. Right, everybody?" and then to his driver "O K, Ledbury, drive off now."

The four vehicles moved off and began to round the shallow corner which led into the southern side of the village square.

"Christ Almighty." Wittmann's vehicle was crossing the square's southern end less than hundred yards distant and Fairclough had never seen a live Tiger that close before.

"Sunray here! Sunray here! Target! Tiger tank. Repeat, Tiger tank. Range 150 yards. 1 o'clock. A P."

Standing in the turret of his Tiger Wittmann saw B Company column begin to drive round the corner. "Woll! Woll! New target. Cromwells entering the square. Fire when on."

The CLY layer and Woll, the most experienced gunner in 101st Battalion, both spun their dials. The Yeoman was faster but was not accurate. The shell from the 17-pdr in Fairclough's Firefly struck the Tiger's turret a glancing blow. Only the thick armour saved it from destruction. Woll's shot hit the Firefly but although it was not a killing shot it halted the column for a few seconds. These few seconds delay were enough for Wittmann. He was a warrior dedicated to battle, but he was at a disadvantage in the present fight. He would pull back.

"Driver. Reverse. Tempo! tempo!" And then once the Tiger was out of immediate danger he ordered it to be turned round and to head for the far side of the square where he would have a better field of fire. Because the Obersturmführer had seen no sign of British infantry his appreciation of the situation was that Villers-Bocage was being held by a British tank group. If he could hold them at bay until the rest of his Company came forward then his few vehicles could drive the Tommy armour out of the village and the flank of Panzer Lehr Division would be secured.

"Mother Tiger to cubs. Where are you? I repeat, where are you? You are needed here - NOW - NOW. Come forward."

Reimers, the driver, locked the Tiger's track and as the vehicle spun it came once again, but only momentarily, into the line of fire of the Firefly gunner. He fired a snap shot which struck and jarred the Tiger, knocking the microphone from Wittmann's hand. He bent down inside the turret to recover it and when he stood up again was horrified to see, only a few yards away, a Cromwell facing him. Captain Lee had moved from the side street and had been stalking the Tiger and had manoeuvred himself so as to shoot it in the back. Lee saw the Tiger turn on its track and realised that his chance of a killing shot through the thinner back armour was gone. But, he reasoned, an armour piercing round fired into the front armour at such close range must surely smash its way through and destroy the enemy machine.

"Gunner: fire" and the solid shot struck the panzer's front. It did not strike through. Captain Lee knew that he and his crew were doomed.

Wittmann's reactions were no less fast.

"Woll! Woll! In front of us - a Cromwell. Fire! Fire!"

Through Lee's mind passed the words of the Grace spoken before meals. "For what we are about to receive may the Lord make us truly grateful," but he did not see the shell smoke pour from the muzzle of the 88 because the solid shot had already struck and destroyed his vehicle. Captain Lee jumped from the turret and another crew member escaped through a hatch. They were the only survivors. The other crewmen lay dead inside the tank, mangled by the shell which whirled around the fighting compartment.

"Crew!! Fuel and ammo state." Wittmann realised that both would have to be replenished if he and his Company were to hold the village. God alone knew when the next opportunity would come. From the turret the Obersturmführer could see that the road rising up towards Point 213 was clear. On it the Tigers of his Company were rolling towards the village and in the distance, up near the crest of the ridge, he could see the Panzergrenadiers of 2nd Panzer Division mopping up the last flickering British resistance. With a fair idea of the enemy tank strength in Villers-Bocage the Obersturmführer was confident that he and his lads could hold it.

Chapter 13

There comes a time when, looking back upon a sequence of events, one can pin-point with a fair degree of accuracy when good fortune begins to come to an end and good luck starts to run out. In Wittmann's case this must surely have been the afternoon of Sunday 13th June, when, after refuelling, he rejoined the two Tigers of his Company and a Panzer IV from Panzer Lehr Division, who were on a standing picquet on the outskirts of Villers-Bocage.

Earlier in the day he had misread British intentions. The Tommies had not, as he had expected them to, stayed in the village but had pushed on uphill towards the high ground. Luck had been with him then so that he had been able to turn this error of judgement to his own advantage. But then, as he led his Company column from the outskirts of Villers-Bocage towards the village square, he made a more serious mistake. This one cost him his own Tiger, a second from his Company and the Panzer IV from the Lehr Division. In Wittmann's own case, although it was not the first time he had had a panzer shot from under him, it was the manner of how this came about which showed that his star, having reached its most glittering height, was faltering - preparing to drop.

The survivors of 22nd Armoured Brigade had not been idle during the time that Wittmann was away refuelling. It was clear to the Brigadier that the Boche tankmen intended to occupy the village in order to hold the left flank of Panzer Lehr. It was equally obvious that the probe which the single Tiger had carried out had been a sort of recce and that when he pulled back, it had only been to bring forward reinforcements. Well, let them come, thought the Brigadier. We are ready for them. He had positioned a Troop of three Cromwells and a Firefly in the square. Any vehicle coming from the direction of Point 213 and driving towards the Caumont road must pass across the top of the square and could be taken in flank. As a back up to the armour the Brigadier had positioned a 6-pdr of the Queens Regiment in an adjacent side street.

Wittmann led his column towards the square. Just ahead was the bend in the Caumont road where the Cromwells had been and he concentrated hard on trying to read the situation. So deep was that concentration that without considering the danger he drove across the open end of the square where the British armour lay in ambush.

"Sunray Major, here." It was the Brigadier on the command set. "The first Tiger is moving across the square. Cromwells, let him pass.

Queens, you shoot him in the side when he passes in front of you. Then the Firefly and the Cromwells can take out the other Boche tanks."

The sound of a 6-pdr firing was like that of a firework compared with the noise of the heavy tank guns. Nor did the 6-pdr have the power to knock out a Tiger except at point blank range. But the Brigadier was determined to kill the Boches who had destroyed his Brigade and had placed his tanks and the anti-tank gun as close as he dared to the route which they must take. The guns of his ambush were so near to the road that conventional sights were useless. Each gun had, therefore, been sighted through the barrel at the house directly opposite. At so close a range, even the 6-pdr must surely gain a 'kill'. The Queens anti-tank gun crew were alert and ready but instinctively, each man took a deep breath at the roar of the Tiger tank, now only yards away. There were only seconds to go. Then the barrel of the 88 appeared. Thank Heaven it was pointing forward in the direction of the Caumont road. Then the turret of the huge panzer came into view and then the wheels and tracks as the vehicle rolled across the top of the narrow street. "Fire." The 6-pdr shell passed clean through the Tiger's side armour and smashed the engine. The vehicle rolled to a halt but before it stopped the Firefly in the square had 'killed' the second Tiger and the Panzer IV had fallen to a Cromwell. Only the third Tiger, which had not entered the square, was able to pull back and make good its escape.

Wittmann's crew had not been wounded by the 6-pdr shell. Emerging from their escape hatches they raced away from the 'dead' vehicle and into a house just off the square. "So far as I know," Wittmann began, "we have no units closer to us than Panzer Lehr and they're about 10 miles away. So it means a long march, but we must get back into action so that we hold the village against the Tommies. Do you all have a firearm? Right, on your feet and let's start moving."

Just over three footsore hours later and Wittmann was in front of Bayerlein, the General Officer Commanding Panzer Lehr Division.

"What's all this about you knocking out twenty-five armoured vehicles in half an hour, Wittmann?" was the General's greeting to the Obersturmführer.

"Well, they weren't all battle tanks, General."

"No matter - a marvellous achievement, Wittmann, truly incredible. Now get your men something to eat and after you have rested a bit you can lead one of my panzer battalions back to Villers-Bocage and organise their attack."

It was twilight when Wittmann and his crew, cramped together in a Kübelwagen, brought a column of Panzer IV back to the ruined village. It was deadly quiet. There were no sounds of firing - nothing at all.

"Obersturmführer Wittmann?" a voice called through the summer night.

"Here...Herr Oberst," as Wittmann recognised the Commanding Officer of one of the 2nd Division's Panzergrenadier Regiments.

"The Tommies have pulled out," the Oberst reported, "and my men have now consolidated their hold on the place. My orders are to send you back to your battalion without delay. Corps has been asking for you. Yours was really a splendid feat of arms. May I be the first to congratulate you."

Wittmann climbed wearily back into the Kübelwagen. "Take me to Battalion HQ, please," and exhausted with the strain of the day he sat slumped in the car, not hearing the thunder of the British guns bombarding Caen nor seeing the flickering lights of the explosions rising and falling on the far horizon. The Kübelwagen driver saw the battalion sign board at the side of the road and swung the car up a long dark lane to stop at a low, camouflaged tent.

"Battalion Headquarters, Obersturmführer."

Outside the tent von Westerhagen was waiting. Tired though he was, Wittmann determined to report in the formal manner. He braced his shoulders and marched towards his superior officer.

"Obersturmführer Wittmann reporting back from battle. I have to report that we have carried out our orders. Villers-Bocage is in our hands and the enemy has been destroyed."

Von Westerhagen took both Wittmann's hands in his own.

"Congratulations, Michael. Reports have been coming in of your effort. A remarkable achievement." He looked with sympathy at the young man standing before him.

"But you are all in. Enough for tonight. We'll talk in the morning and then you can write your report on today's splendid achievement - Oh, by the by. Woll has been with you, hasn't he, acting as your gunner while his own Tiger was being repaired? Well, it is ready now so tomorrow morning, first thing, he returns to his Company. The man who will replace him is Sturmmann Wagner, a good man. You'll meet him tomorrow, too. Now, Michael, turn in and sleep well. God knows you've earned a long rest."

Chapter 14

Michael Wittmann's almost single-handed action in destroying 22nd Armoured Brigade, the advance guard of the 'Desert Rats', had at strategic level the consequence that Montgomery's plan for the development of the Normandy campaign was brought to naught. At a personal level it brought Wittmann a recommendation for the Swords to the Oak Leaves of the Knights Cross.

'Sepp' Dietrich, the General Officer Commanding 1st SS Panzer Corps, was not a literary genius but he did know how to write a citation that would appeal to Hitler. Part of the citation which he drafted to recommend Wittmann read:

"The situation demanded immediate action. There was no time for Wittmann to brief his men. Instead he climbed into his Tiger and charged into battle, firing at the English column. By his prompt action the enemy tanks were first separated...He then drove down the column and destroyed the vehicles in it. The other four Tigers of his Company took 230 prisoners. With his Tiger shot into immobility under him he continued to destroy all the enemy close at hand...before carrying out a foot march of some 15kms to gain touch with Panzer Lehr Division. Then, heading a column of Panzer IV's in his Schwimmwagen, he drove back into Villers-Bocage. He met the remaining panzers of his Company and planned their attack upon the town..."

Action upon Dietrich's recommendation was swift and the document passed through the high echelons of Command to even more senior ones and, finally, to the Supreme Commander himself. Back down through the hierarchical structure came the Führer Order and it landed at last on the desk of Wittmann's immediate superior, von Westerhagen.

"Runner"

"Obersturmbannführer?"

"My compliments to Obersturmführer Wittmann. Ask him to report to me, please."

Minutes later Wittmann stood in front of the Battalion Commander.

"Michael," began Westerhagen. "I have here an order for you to go to Berlin. From there you will proceed to Rastenburg and report to the Führer in his Headquarters there. In Rastenburg you are to be presented with the Swords to the Oak Leaves. Congratulations, Michael. We are all proud of you. Corps is sending a car to take you to the airport. It will be coming for you in an hour."

Wittmann's journey to Rastenburg was a kaleidoscope of various methods of transport and of a bewildering number of strange faces. First there was the journey by fast car through France to a military airfield outside Paris, then the flight by a He111K to the Reich's capital and then from Berlin's Gatow airport a third leg, by Ju52, to the Wolf's Lair. Another fast car drive and then at the perimeter of the Lair a personal body-search by SS officers, none of whom, he noticed, had any combat decorations. As Wittmann entered an ante-room the buzz of conversation among the senior commanders stopped and was replaced by the sibilant whispering of his name. One of the SS officers on equerry duty in the Lair gave him a quick briefing on the etiquette of presentation and then the door to the Führer's study was flung open to admit him. Ramrod stiff, the Obersturmführer marched into the centre of the room and halted at the regulation five paces distance from the Führer.

"Obersturmführer Wittmann, reporting as ordered, mein Führer."

Hitler came close to him and shook his hand with a firm grip.

"We have, of course, met before, Obersturmführer, but before we go on to the formal part of the ceremony let me tell you that I have known your family for years. Your father and I served in the same battalion of 12th Bavarian Infantry Regiment during the Great War. You look so much like him you could almost be him, as he was all those years ago. Yes, it's true," Hitler went on as he saw the surprise in the officer's face. "There is in fact a photograph taken in Flanders in which your father and I are shown as part of a small group. Under normal circumstances your family would have been invited to be present, but war-time conditions change so many things. I am also sorry that neither General Hausser nor General Dietrich can be present, but as you well know the fighting in Normandy does not allow them to be here today. Did you know that Brigadeführer Witt was killed in action the other day? Such a sad loss…I have appointed Meyer, you know him better as Panzermeyer, so I am told, to be the new commander of the 'Hitler Youth' Division. There have been other changes in command and promotions, apropos of which, you have been raised to the rank of Hauptsturmführer. Please accept my sincerest congratulations. But I am anticipating events. Let us begin the ceremony." The Führer nodded and at that signal the equerries moved to their positions.

A voice from somewhere behind Wittmann's right shoulder read the citation. Hitler stood impassive, his hands folded in front of him until the voice stopped reading. An SS equerry moved forward and opened the lid of a small, square, black box. Inside lay the insignia. Hitler took it out and held the cross in his hand until another equerry had fastened the ribbon at the back of Wittmann's neck. There was a second handshake from the Führer and a few more words of thanks before Wittmann turned and marched out of the room. As the door closed behind him he was greeted by the applause of the commanders in the ante-room. Flushing with embarrassment at this demonstration on the part of his superiors he walked quickly into a low-ceilinged map room, without noticing the group of officers gathered round the situation maps on the walls.

"Hauptsturmführer," called a thin, high voice. The voice was unmistakable and Wittmann turned to look into the face of Heinrich Himmler, the Supreme Commander of the whole SS organisation.

"Reichsführer?" He asked.

"Let me first congratulate you on the award you have been given and your well-deserved promotion," began Himmler. He took off his pince-nez and began to polish the lens glasses. With them cleaned to his satisfaction he looked directly at the young officer.

"Now comes the question of your future employment in the SS," he went on. "I have suggested to the Führer and he has accepted my suggestion that you be withdrawn from front-line service and given a senior post in a training establishment. You can then pass on to the new boys the lessons of your vast, one might say, unique, combat experience in Russia and in France..."

The Reichsführer SS stopped talking as he saw Wittmann slowly shake his head. "The instruction you could give would be invaluable," he began again, but then stopped as he saw the same slow shake of the head.

"With respect, Reichsführer," Wittmann countered. "I am a soldier not a teacher. Therefore, although I may not know how to instruct, I do know to fight. Indeed, only in battle do I feel that I am playing my full part in the nation's struggle. I would beg you, please, do not force me to take up the post of an instructor. Even the prospects of promotion could not induce me to take it on. At this time, in Normandy and on the Eastern Front, it is warriors that Germany needs."

"I had anticipated that that would be your answer, Wittmann," Himmler beamed, "and I am pleased to hear it. Of course you can go back to active service but before you do, you have a very long period of leave due to you. You live in Bavaria, don't you?...I shall arrange transport."

"Yes, I am Bavarian" replied Wittmann, "but I shall not be very long with the family on our farm..." Nor was he, but spent a week of furlough fretting and willing the days to pass quickly. At last the time came when he could stand the inaction no longer and he made preparations to return to the place which had replaced Bavaria as his Home - the battlefield. He had been away for only a brief time and when he returned he found both the 12th SS Panzer Division (Hitler Youth) and his 101st Tiger Battalion, which was supporting the 12th, under severe pressure and fighting against overwhelming odds.

Chapter 15

Montgomery's battle plan was not running well. Falaise, key to the break out and exploitation phase of his grand strategic design, and that city which he had expected to take within days was, in August, still in German hands. He decided on a fresh offensive to capture the town. The plan, code-named 'Totalise', was laid out on 3rd August and the intention of General Simonds to whom Montgomery had passed the attack order, and whose 2nd Canadian Corps would carry out the assault, was for a massive blow straight down the N158. Simonds' briefing to his senior commanders was direct and straightforward. "Montgomery has ordered us to capture Falaise without delay. If...No..." he corrected himself quickly. "When - when we take it the possibility exists that we may have trapped the entire German 7th Army in a huge pocket. That is why it is important that this offensive succeeds." He paused for effect and looked at the faces of his divisional commanders and their staffs. Years of military training kept their eyes blank and their faces expressionless but the Corps Commander could guess the doubts they felt and he had already anticipated in his mind the type of question they would raise.

"Corps will mount a night assault striking down the road from Caen to Falaise - here" he pointed to the N158 which ran in an almost dead straight line. "The 51st Highland, with 33rd Armoured Brigade in support, will thrust down the eastern side of that road. The 2nd Canadian Infantry Division, with 2nd Canadian Armoured Brigade in support, will advance down the west side of the road. Any questions so far?" He paused. No one spoke.

"Right," he went on. "The objectives of 51st Highland Division are St. Aignan and Cramesnil by 1130hrs on 7th August. The Jocks will consolidate. Then at 1400hrs on the 8th the 1st Polish Armoured Division will pass through 51st who will, by that time, have broken the enemy. The Poles will belt hell for leather to Falaise." He stopped talking and looked around the faces.

"All clear, so far?" Nobody spoke. "Right. The 4th Canadian Armoured Division will pass through 2nd Canadian Infantry Division and will seize the high ground to the west of the main road so as to support the Polish advance. In particular 4th Armoured will seize the hills between Potigny and the Laize valley. Those, gentlemen, are the intentions. Now, you are asking yourselves what sort of cock-up will be produced by night attack and you will also be asking why am I using two unblooded Divisions in the exploitation stage of the battle."

Simonds' anticipation had been correct.

These were the thoughts that had entered the minds of many of those in the room. Night attacks were always fraught with problems and it was true that neither 4th Canadian Armoured nor the 1st Polish Armoured had yet been in battle.

"The assault battalions of the 51st Highland will be brought forward in Kangaroos, that is to say "Priest" AFVs which have been converted into armoured personnel carriers. As I said, the Kangaroos will bring the assault battalions right up to their form-up lines. The infantry will then debus and mount their attacks. Their task is to open the way forward for the armour which will pass through and thrust down to Falaise. All the tactical details will be supplied within two days, OK? Oh, yes. And why unblooded Divisions - well, we were all unblooded once and, once Ritchie's 51st has smashed a way through, then exploitation should be a piece of cake. Now, what I want to show you is this." Simonds pulled back a curtain to show a battle map.

"The arrows are SS Panzer Divisions on the American sector. Hitler has ordered them to seal off the base of the Cotentin peninsula, here at Mortain," he pointed to the place. "They haven't a hope in hell - you and I know that - but while the SS Panzer Divisions are away we can make our play. I have every confidence that we shall succeed. I hope you, too, are confident and that you can fill your men with the same spirit. This time we'll do it. Questions? No? Thank you, gentlemen."

Details of the attack were given in O Groups all the way down the military chain. The 7th Argylls held their O group in Cormelles and when it was finished the Platoon Commanders went back to the bivouac areas to brief their men on the part that their battalion would play in the forthcoming battle.

"Everybody here, Sergeant Veitch?"

"Sir." The men of Tony Lamont's Platoon were seated on the grass in front of him. "Right. Corps will attack tomorrow - 7th August. The 154th Brigade will go in with ourselves and 1st Black Watch up. The 7th Black Watch will be in reserve, behind us…Who said cushy bastards?" His men laughed. It was an old joke. "We'll be riding into the attack in Kangaroos, which will take us almost onto the objective. Each battalion will form an attack column four vehicles wide. OK so far?"

There was no response. It was all very familiar stuff to the veterans and as for the rookies, they did not dare ask for fear of being

TOM RITCHIE WAS MAJ.GEN. COMMADING MY DIVISION

THE 3R BRITISH ASSAULT DIV ON 'D' DAY HE WAS WOUNDED ON 13 JUNE AND ON HIS RETURN WAS GIVEN COMMAND OF THE 51ST HIGHLAND DIV WHICH HAD FOUGHT IN N.AFRICA SCIULLY & ITALY ridiculed.

"The Pioneer Platoon," Lamont went on, "will put out shaded hurricane lamps to light the route. Those of you who were at Alamein will remember them. The NCOs will explain how these work to the new boys after this O Group. Our column colour is green, so drivers, as long as you see a green light you are on the right track. Our Kangaroos will also carry a dimmed tail light." He halted again, "Everything clear?" There was a dead silence.

"Once we debus Bofors will fire tracer down our flanks to show direction and green smoke will be fired - not that that is likely to do anything but bugger us up." He waited for the embarrassed laugh. The men could not get accustomed to him using such common language. "Once on our objective, it's a little village, the Poles come through and take up the running. Now," and his voice changed from familiarity and took on the tone of a commander, "...the CO has told me to emphasise - we are the lead Battalion of the Brigade and our Brigade is the spearhead of the Divisional attack. It's a great honour to be selected," he waited for the usual groan which greeted that cliché and spoke over it. "We lead the Battalion. Our Battalion leads the Brigade and our Brigade leads the Division. So our role is vital. Speed is essential and we go in under a barrage which will lift 100 yards every minute. Now..." he stopped again and tried to infuse into his voice a feeling of optimism. "Monty wants THIS Division to do the job of opening up the road to Falaise, just as we opened up things at Alamein. He wants us because he knows that the 51st can do it. The Division Commander wants our Brigade to lead because we're the best and the Brigade has chosen us to be one of the two assault battalions. It's a big honour so let's be worthy of it."

After the briefing a pair of NCOs walked back to their bivvy - a two man tent set up over a slit trench; a necessary precaution employed by units which were within range of German artillery.

"Well, Tommy, what d'ye think?"

Corporal Tommy Logan paused briefly, spat and moved on again. "It'll be the usual balls-up, you mark my words. All this blathering about illuminated signs marking the track. Once the shit starts flying a lot of notice the drivers'll take of them and if - it's a big if - we can get by compass bearing to the form-up line, can you imagine the shambles? No," the Corporal repeated cynically, "It'll be like every other cock-up. D'ye mind all the other times when we've been told how easy it'll be?"

Tommy Logan and Lance-Corporal Douglas Fraser stopped to take in the fading light of a beautiful summer's evening, listening to the sounds which came to them. "Aye, a real cock up, is what it'll be Dougie," and Corporal Logan sighed reflectively. "Just like all the others."

And he was right. The bombing raid which commenced at 2300hrs, by more than a thousand Lancasters and Halifaxes, created so much dust and smoke that the Master Bomber aborted the attacks by the final squadrons so that these, one third of the whole force, jettisoned their bomb loads in the English Channel. And most of the machines which did drop their loads onto the battlefield, bombed too early - and their loads fell on allied troops. This event produced the joyful rumour in one of the two Regiments of the German 89th Division that the Luftwaffe had, at long last, entered the battle for Normandy. No such pleasure was felt by the other Regiment of the 89th Division which was holding the ground to the west of the Falaise road. Its positions, from the outpost line to well past Regimental HQ, were smothered in a hail of bombs and the formation was all but destroyed. Those who survived the raid - and they were few - were shaken and panicky.

The raid ended well before midnight. Already at 2200hrs the Kangaroo columns had begun to form up south of Cormelles. "Sunray Major here." Toby Nicholson commanding 'A' Squadron of a regiment in the Armoured Brigade was calling up the component units of his column.

"Ready for the off, all units. Navigators OK ? Report in. Over."

"Affirmative, Sunray Major," came from the navigators in the two tank Troops.

"Flails ?"

"OK Sunray Major."

"Sappers ?"

"Ready to move."

"Argylls ?"

"Ready, Sunray."

Nicholson stood up in the turret of his Sherman, peered into the darkness ahead, turned round and looked into the night behind him. Six hundred yards his column stretched; three hundred in front of him and three hundred behind. His task was to get this mass of vehicles to the debussing point at the right time. He began to sweat a little - not from fear but from the responsibility. So much could go wrong. He ducked down inside the turret and checked the time by torchlight. Twenty two forty eight hours.

Ready for the off. The feeling was like that before riding in a hard point to point. Willing the race to start yet wondering what would happen when it did. He stood up again in the turret and adjusted the neck microphone.

"Sunray Major to all. Move now," and to his driver. "Right, Johnston, advance."

The engine noise increased in volume as the Shermans heading the column moved off. Fifty yards ahead the first shaded hurricane lamp glowed green in the darkness. Prompt at 2250hrs the lead vehicle of the column crossed the form-up line and as it did so searchlights, positioned miles behind the British front lines, opened up so that their beams shining onto the clouds created an eerie, milky glow - "Monty's Moonlight."

The column was still out of sight of Waldmüller's outpost line but the rattle and roar of the tanks carried well on the still night air. The Grenadier officers walked from fox-hole to fox-hole. "Keep your nerve, lads. The Tommies can't see you, but you can see them. Let the tanks through - the second line will take them out with panzerfausts. Your task is to kill the Tommy infantry. Keep calm, lads, keep calm."

The Grenadiers, children in years, but already battle-hardened veterans, knew that not until the enemy barrage crashed down need they worry, for Tommy's tanks did not advance without their covering barrage and that fire hadn't started yet. They did not have long to wait. Far away to the north, clearly visible even in the pale white of the searchlight beams, yellow flashes lit up the sky. Seven hundred British guns had opened up and only seconds later the whistling as the projectiles passed through the air ended in a series of crashing explosions. Sturmmann Glocke looked over the edge of his slit trench. "Lovely," he exulted, "Fifty metres in front." He knew from experience that British barrages were calculated in 100 metre 'lifts'. Barring bad luck from shells falling short, the next salvo must, therefore, fall behind the trench line. He ducked down to the bottom of the slit, covered his head in the camouflage jacket and lit a cigarette. The first puff calmed him. There was nothing to do now but wait.

Major Nicholson was not so relaxed. Positioned halfway down the right hand column he realised that its length was increasing. This lengthening had begun almost as soon as the first tanks had crossed the start line and, as the column drove towards the objective, smoke and dust had created an opaque curtain. Then one of the flail tanks knocked over a number of green signal lamps and the following AFVs had milled about until an officer led them on foot back to their track. Nicholson knew that it was useless for him to order the column to close up. Cohesion depended upon the bravery of the tank drivers and if this blinding fog made them a bit hesitant, then all his orders would not improve matters. Something strange was happening. Although he could not see the ground Nicholson could feel from the way that his tank lurched from one crater to another that it was badly broken up. He knew that 25-pdrs could not make such deep holes. Oh God, the realisation struck him. These were bomb craters. The RAF had not hit the target. They had dropped their bombs short so that they had fallen across the ground over which his squadron was advancing. They would cause delays; bad delays.

A babble of voices came over the air. "Sunray! Sunray !" Tank crews reported that three of the lead tanks and a flail had 'bellied' in a deep crater and could not get out. One of the three carried a navigator and he had suffered concussion when the vehicle turned over. Another crisis...Again came the call "Sunray! Sunray!" but Nicholson did not need to ask what was happening. It was only too clear. The column had bumped the enemy. Spandau tracer flying slowly towards the vehicles, seemed suddenly to gain speed in its approach and whistled overhead to fade away into the dark night. The column had not even reached the debussing point and already it was under fire.

"Sunray to Argylls....Dismount." The Highlanders swung themselves over the walls of the Kangaroos and stood waiting for orders. The Shermans moved on but were soon halted again by an embankmented railway line. The tanks cruised about looking for a crossing point. Nicholson felt frustration creating a lump in his throat which threatened to choke him. His tanks could not swan around without infantry protection in the middle of the night and in enemy territory. It was too dangerous. He needed infantry back up. He knew that the Jocks would accuse him of buggering them about but it had to be done.

"Sunray here. Argylls embus. Come forward." He was ordering them into a firework display of deadly beauty. The night sky was criss-crossed with lines of shining beads; machine gun tracer and most of it German. As the SS officers had told the Grenadiers, they could see the enemy but the tank gunners could not see them and could only fire at where they thought the SS soldiers were. Hours late, with the battle's time table badly adrift, the 51st Highland began to reach the battlefield. Not until 0400hrs did parts of the right hand column arrive at the debussing point. B Company, the first to make the objective, debussed, shook out into formation and opened its attack. A

Company, whose Kangaroo drivers had lost contact in a thick night-time mist, came to the debussing point in penny packets. When D Company arrived it was moved forward to beef up A Company's attack. The delay in the Argylls reaching the debussing points meant that it was already light before the two Highland Companies opened their attack, marching silently through a dense, morning mist towards Cramesnil.

Sturmmann Glocke peered through the cold curtain of fog towards where he knew the village to be. There was a great deal of noise coming from it. A sudden gust of wind dispersed the mist curtain briefly but it had been long enough for him to see figures wearing flat helmets and brown uniforms - Tommies. "There they are." he shouted and pointed. "Have I permission to open fire, Scharführer?" and anticipating the NCO's assent, poured a stream of bullets into 'A' Company. The first burst killed the Company Commander and wounded most of the HQ group. The rapid fire coming out of the mist shook the Highlanders but a subaltern held the platoons together and led them in a charge to take out the Spandaus. Corporal Lindsay fired a burst from his Sten and Glocke fell dead over the butt of his MG42. The Argylls fought their way through the village. The Jerry crust must have surely been cracked. It was time to call forward the supporting armour. Nicholson's Squadron had suffered heavy losses in its advance. Eight of the vehicles which had penetrated the Grenadier outpost line had been knocked out by panzerfausts and the tank crews, already twitchy, were becoming neurotic. Any bloody Jerry might have a rocket about him and Cramesnil was crawling with the bastards.

"Sunray Major here." It was the Commanding Officer of the Argylls. "Sandy, send out a patrol towards the road and gain touch with our chums on the right flank."

"Wilco, Sunray Major. Out...". B Company commander, now in charge not only of his own Company but also of the leaderless A, sent out a recce group. He wiped a grimy hand across his face. The attack had not gone well. The column had bumped Jerry earlier than had been expected and cohesion had been lost. Thank Heaven, casualties had not been too heavy, but it had been a real dog's breakfast. The bloody tanks had let us down yet again, he concluded viciously.

In a freshly dug slit trench Corporal Logan and Lance-Corporal Fraser sat smoking. "What did I tell you, Dougie. A right cock-up. We'll no take Falaise today." Logan had already prophesied one event correctly. His second prophecy was also to come true. Falaise did not fall that day. Allied Intelligence had wrongly forecast that the 12th SS Division would be employed with the other SS Panzer Divisions in the Mortain attack. But it was not, and the Hitler Youth was still there on the ground in front of Falaise, with its organisation largely intact and with its Grenadiers waiting for the events of the day to unfold. Their training had taught them that an enemy attack would be followed by their own counter-attack. Well, the Tommies had launched an attack and had punched a small salient into the outpost line held by Waldmüller's Grenadiers. It was clear that part of the Regiment must soon be committed to action to drive back the Tommies. Orders must come soon, but until they did, the thing to do for any sensible Grenadier was to lie down and rest and wait for the boys from B Echelon to bring a hot breakfast forward into the front line. And so the Grenadiers waited cocooned in the clinging white mist of an Autumn morning waiting for food and for the counter-attack which they knew would be mounted. Well, it was a nice day for it.

Chapter 16

"Hauptsturmführer!!"

Reimers did not need to shake the sleeping commander a second time. With the swift reactions of a front-line soldier Wittmann was awake and instantly alert.

"What is it?"

"The Divisional Commander has come forward on a recce. He has left word. He presents his compliments and you are to meet him in half an hour in Bretteville," then noticing the puzzled look on his superior's face, he added, "That is Bretteville-sur-Glaize and not Bretteville-le-Rabet, of course."

Wittmann looked at his watch. Nearly six o'clock. It was a misty and chilly morning but with a countryman's knowledge he knew that the day would soon be hot and sunny. Half an hour gave him time to wash and to swill down a mug of coffee while he was shaving. There would be time enough to drive forward to meet Panzermeyer. Mentally he ran over the route that allied superiority in the air would force him to take. Up the N158 to Cintheaux, turn left to Quilly and follow the road round to Bretteville. It was a pity that he could not go across country, but if he did he would be in the open and a sitting target for any allied fighter-bomber cruising overhead. Going by the route he had worked out in his mind was certainly a long way round, but the bocage lanes and trees provided cover from detection and, therefore, protection from air attack. Small vehicles scurrying quickly through arches of trees often escaped detection and attack, but large and immobile targets like villages and towns could not. There had been no cover and protection for Bretteville and yesterday's bombing raid had flattened it. Within ten minutes of having been wakened, Wittmann was on the road and in Bretteville he found Panzermeyer on the 'enemy' side of the ruined village with his car parked some distance from the piles of rubble that had once been houses. The Divisional Commander was standing in a clump of trees looking through binoculars at the ground in front of him.

"Good morning, Oberführer."

Panzermeyer took the glasses from his eyes.

"Good morning, Wittmann. I had to come up and see the situation for myself. The most confusing reports have been coming in to Div Headquarters. The 89th Division, our left flank neighbour, is said to have crumbled. The pasting they took in yesterday's bombing raid is said to have shaken them badly. If there's another bombing raid like that today then the 89th will certainly break. As it is, the Tommies are reported to be through the 89th's main defence line, but so far as I can gather there are still some strong points holding out and stopping the Tommy advance. God alone knows what is happening over in Rocquancourt and May," he gestured with his head to where the villages lay mist-shrouded, less than two kilometres away.

"Garcelles is supposed to be still in our hands," the Oberführer pointed to the low ridge on the far side of the N158, still hidden in the light morning mist, "But in St Aignan the Tommies have been pushing through all night. We are out of radio contact with most of our units and none of the runners I've sent out have come back yet." Panzermeyer was worried. The N158, running from Caen to Falaise, was crucial to the defence plans of Army Group B and Army Group had given his 'Hitler Youth' Division the task of stopping the allies advancing down that road. His young lads had been in action for weeks without relief and were suffering from battle exhaustion. Corps had said that 85th Infantry Division was coming into the line to relieve his Division but when the 85th would arrive and in what shape, was anybody's guess. How long this Army mob would be able to withstand the massed allied tank attacks and bombing raids was even more questionable. It might very well go the way of the 89th, with units breaking up in panic. By God, it was a worrying time but he had been given orders to stand and hold the Tommies and both he and the SS 'Hitler Youth' Division would stand, as ordered.

In silence the two men surveyed the battleground. The August sun was beginning to warm the soil and, even as they watched, some villages and farms began to emerge from the mist, shining and clear in the growing light while others still remained stubbornly hidden. A motor cycle DR roared up.

"Company Commander's compliments, Oberführer. He thinks you should know that the Army Commander has come into our area. He's in Urville."

"Thank you, we'll go immediately. Had breakfast yet, lad? No? Then go to the cookhouse in Div HQ and tell them I said to feed you. Wittmann, come with me, please."

General Eberbach, commanding 5th Panzer Army, was standing, partially hidden, in the shade of some oaks and was quartering the ground professionally through his binoculars. "Good morning Meyer. Good morning, Wittmann. God, what would I give to know how today will end. I tell you, gentlemen, I have the gravest fears. The enemy's material superiority is frightening..."

"That may well be," Panzermeyer broke in, cockily determined not to let the Army man see how anxious he himself was. "But we have the better morale. One of my Grenadiers said yesterday when that big air raid came in, that Churchill had paid us the greatest compliment. He had sent each of us in the Division the present of a personal bomber to wipe us out. Don't worry, General, my men will hold," and then in an off-hand way, "Can't speak for the 89th, of course."

Eberbach, stung by the SS Commander's criticism of an Army unit, turned back to surveying the ground ahead of him. When he had finished he turned to the SS Commander again. "What are your intentions, Meyer?"

The Commander of 12th SS went over the plan he had formulated in his mind. If the front were to break and the troops had to fall back to a new defensive line, then that line needed to be set up without delay. The villages which would form the strong points had to be prepared NOW, in the event of a collapse of the front. The next possible defensive positions were formed by the high ground behind the Laison river and on both sides of Potigny. But the key to the present battle was Cintheaux and the ridge on which the village stood. That commanding position had to be held at all costs and he was prepared to commit every man to holding it. Since, in his opinion, the best form of defence was attack, then the easiest way to upset the Tommies was to launch a pre-emptive assault. They fought the war according to 'gentlemen's hours' and their main tank attacks seldom came in before midday. Between first light and midday Tommy would be methodically preparing for battle and a short, sharp attack by a 'Hitler Youth' Battle Group would knock him off balance and upset his time-table. With that achieved and capitalising upon the enemy's confusion the defence line on either side of Potigny could then be prepared and set up.

"My intention," Meyer concluded, "is to commit Waldmüller's Grenadier Battle Group into an attack to take the high ground to the south of St Aignan. That attack will be spearheaded by Wittmann's Tigers. As you know, General, he is acting as Battalion Commander in the absence of von Westerhagen, who is ill..."

The noise of a motor engine broke into Panzmeyer's explanation. A Kübelwagen carrying the Divisional Adjutant drew up. The officer leaped from the vehicle and flipped open his notebook.

"Orders from Corps, Oberführer. We are to mount an attack as soon as possible to retake the high ground to the south of St Aignan. The 2nd Panzer Battalion will be used to 'lift' a grenadier battle group from Waldmüller's Battalion onto the objective. The Corps Escort Company, together with a Company of the Anti-Tank Battalion will take the heights to the west of St Sylvain. Wünsche's Panzer Battle Group is to break off its operations at Grimbosq and Brieux and move to hold the high ground to the north and north-west of Potigny and the gap between Laison and Laize. The Divisional Artillery and Flak are to support the attack and then to form an PAK front. The attack is to begin no later than 1230hrs."

Meyer listened attentively and then turned to Eberbach. "Great minds think alike, eh General?" and then in the formal tone that was used between a subordinate and his superior, "Do you give me permission to undertake the attack along the lines that Corps has laid down?"

"Certainly, Oberführer, and the best of luck."

"Right," Meyer turned to the adjutant. "Make a note of time and place for the War Diary. Wittmann! Let's get back. I shan't go to Div HQ but shall stay forward with Waldmüller's group ready to deal with any emergencies that come up. I don't think you need to be at O group. You know the details of the attack already. But I shall come across for a last minute briefing before the 'off'.

Back among his Tigers, Wittmann felt more at ease. He knew he would never make a senior commander moving pins on a map, nor would he make a middle ranker. He would always stay a subaltern. He needed to be among his men, leading them in battle and in person. That was his element. Let the others have their red stripes and golden gorget patches. He was satisfied with his rank and his position. That thought reminded him of the orders that Panzermeyer had given. As acting CO of the 101st SS Heavy Panzer Battalion Wittmann would have to direct the battle from Tiger 007; the Command panzer. The Hauptsturmführer hated the thought. The wireless sets in the Command panzer took up so much space that the vehicle carried fewer than the normal number of rounds for its 88mm main armament. The lack of those 30 shells might be crucial in a hard fought battle. Hate it or not, today he would have to comply with orders and ride in 007. Panzermeyer, the Divisional Commander, needed to be in touch with him at every stage of the battle.

Chapter 17

By mid-morning all traces of mist had cleared. Visibility was perfect for this day of battle. Too perfect, thought Panzermeyer. With this visibility, my lads will be able to see for themselves just how badly outnumbered they are by the Tommy armour. It could make them a bit jumpy. It was a sight that almost unnerved him and he was a veteran of the Eastern Front and of the Red Army's massed tank assaults. In Russia those attacks had been made by whole regiments of armoured fighting vehicles, but here in Normandy, the Tommies had massed entire Divisions to win the battle. Meyer and Waldmüller stood on the top of the long ridge at Cintheaux looking down at the low ground before them which was covered by enemy armour.

"There's a devil of a lot of them," began Waldmüller, at last breaking the silence. As far as his eye could see the fields on the western side of the N158 were packed with armour - tanks, troop carriers, SP's and scout cars. Confident - arrogant - in the knowledge of allied air superiority, the enemy artillery regiments were deployed on open ground, the gunners not even bothering to cover the guns with camouflage netting. The noise of hundreds of tank engines warming up for battle reverberated on the morning air. There was little shellfire and what there was came mostly from enemy batteries ranging themselves in.

"As I see it," Panzermeyer said, once he had considered the situation for a last time. "The enemy armoured group in St Aignan is the weakest of the three on our sector. The lot around Cramesnil looks the most dangerous and under normal circumstances it is the one which I would have attacked first."

"But," he commented bitterly, "These are not normal circumstances. If only we had time to pick and choose our objectives! Ah well. My orders from Corps are to 'lift' your Grenadiers onto St Aignan and the wood to the east of Garcelles. The bulk of our panzer force will take your lads in and 2nd Panzer Battalion will stay with you. A small panzer detachment under Wittmann will come back from Garcelles and will attack the Tommies on the western side of the road and then go on to beat back the lot at Cramesnil."

"What I can't understand," remarked Waldmüller, "Is why the Tommies have made no attack yet. God knows they have numbers on their side. What are they waiting for?"

"Surely you know their methods by now, Sturmbannführer. They are waiting for another bombing raid to go in before their tanks make any sort of advance."

The two officers concentrated upon the battlefield, working out lines of approach and searching for dead ground. Their concentration was broken by the appearance of a single RAF bomber which approached the area and began to circle above it. "Their flying HQ," remarked Panzermeyer, "First he comes - then some time later the massed bombers will appear."

And there they were. Still many miles away, so far away indeed that they were nothing more than black dots in the north-western sky. The enemy's air weapon, forming a seemingly unending procession of heavy bombers, was approaching the target area. The aircraft of the American Air Force always flew in such perfect formation that they were known to the German Army in Normandy as the 'Party Day Parade', a reference to the Luftwaffe fly-pasts on ceremonial Nazi Party occasions in pre-war Germany. The disposition of the black dots in the sky showed that this group was no exception. This was another 'Party Day Parade'.

"Almighty God," breathed Waldmüller, shaking his head in disbelief, "There are hundreds of them. It's overwhelming."

"Yes, it is," agreed Panzermeyer. "But they have a defect. Their bombing procedure is too rigid. They do not bomb a target but a target area. The commanding officer flies in the lead machine and when he gives the order to bomb, they all let go in one massive load, irrespective of whether he is short of the target or has overshot it."

"To be in the area when that load of shit explodes must be hell..."

"It is, so we don't stay to be bombed. Instead we move out of the area and come back again after the aircraft have flown away. It is fairly obvious that today's target for the Tommy planes is Cintheaux. So we move forward out of the village and get as close as we can to the Tommy armour. The nearer we get to them the safer we shall be. It is a nuisance but it does mean we shall have to change the battle plan."

"In what way?"

"We bring forward the time of the attack. In that way our lads will be out of the target area and in the open before the bombers drop their eggs. The objectives remain the same - only the attack time is changed. Right, let's go across to brief Wittmann and then get your lads into the attack. We've not much time before the Tommy bombers get here."

Wittmann stood musing by the side of the bocage hedge, his eyes staring, unfocussed, across the Normandy countryside and his brain only half registering the noises coming from the Command set. The head of Hirschel, the wireless operator appeared suddenly in the turret. "Message from the Divisional Commander. The attack time has been brought forward. He is coming across with Sturmbannführer Waldmüller." Wittmann acknowledged the message absently and then a newer noise intruded upon his thoughts...aircraft engines. With a sinking heart he looked up and saw the enemy bombers approaching the battlefield. Today, then, would be a repetition of yesterday. First the aircraft would crater the ground, then a concentrated barrage would be fired and behind that would come the British armour and infantry. The enemy's methods were so predictable that they were almost a ritual.

~

The Kübelwagen holding Panzermeyer and Waldmüller pulled to a halt by the high hedge on the eastern side of the N158. The two men pushed their way through a narrow gap in the hedge and walked to where Wittmann was standing.

"Hauptsturmführer, the attack must roll before they," Meyer gestured towards the oncoming armada of aeroplanes, "Before they reach us. There's no doubt about it we're the targets. Mount up now. You know the objective and the order of priorities?"

Wittmann nodded. "The group at St Aignan first, then the group on the west side of the road and then the lot at Cramesnil."

"That's correct; in that order. Once the bombers have gone I'll bring the fuel and ammunition trucks up to the southern side of Cintheaux. They'll be in cover on the reverse slope. Oh, yes," and, almost as an afterthought, he added, "The Regimental First Aid Post will be set up there, too." He stopped talking to look at the enemy bomber fleet. It was wheeling, a great mass of silver aeroplanes still holding perfect formation and circling overhead, making sure that the target had been correctly identified.

"Waldmüller, get your men moving. Wittmann, good luck." The three men shook hands. Around the area whistles blew, rousing the Grenadiers and ordering them into formation. Wittmann swung himself onto the side of Tiger 007, climbed into the turret and lowered himself onto the seat in the fighting compartment. He picked up the Command set microphone. There was a loud crackle of static in the earphones.

"All crews, all crews. Mother Tiger here. The objectives are: One, the wood to the east of Garcelles. We shall take the Grenadiers as far as that point, they will dismount and comb the wood. The bulk of our

Battalion will stay with them. Target two: Cubs Albert, Bodo, Caesar and Dora will return with me to attack the Tommies on the main road. Target three: My group will head north to halt the Tommy attack at Cramesnil. RV for fuel and ammo - south side of Cintheaux. All crews, all crews...Marsch."

He stood up in the turret to see the Battalion move off. Ahead of his column were little knots of men, the Grenadiers of Waldmüller's Battle Group. Soon the Tigers would reach the foot soldiers and would halt to allow them to clamber on the outsides of the vehicles. The Grenadiers holding on to any foothold they could find, would be carried into the attack upon the Garcelles woods. Wittmann looked up at the noise which blanketed out even the roaring and clattering of his own panzer. The sky seemed to be filled with huge aircraft, but already black puffs of exploding flak shells were causing the rigid formation to break up. The anti-aircraft gunners of the 'Hitler Youth' were concentrating their fire on the first box of Flying Fortresses. The gunners had learned that in an American attack the lead aircraft of the first formation carried the Master Bomber. The flak gunners had only to terrify the crew of that machine and they would panic and drop their bombs. It meant in this case that the bomb loads would fall on allied troops and not on German ones or even the objective. As Wittmann looked up he could see that flak bursts already smothered the Master Bomber. Then it was hit and as it fell the bombardier in the Fortress jettisoned the bomb load. His action threw the whole raid into disarray. More than half of the armada followed the leader's action and dropped their bombs. They fell short of the target.

Through binoculars Wittmann saw the other 'boxes' of aircraft flying in and saw their bomb doors open slowly. It was clear that the follow-up groups were aware of the mistake that had been made and were flying on through the flak determined to drop their bombs on the correct target - the German-held village of Cintheaux. Wittmann saw the clouds of smoke from the explosions rise in the air from the area on which the Canadian tank formations were waiting, and he rejoiced. This unexpected disruption to the Tommies' plans would make the imminent battle a lot easier for his Battalion to fight.

Chapter 18

While the Tiger crews washed, ate and rested, 'A' Echelon teams loaded the racks with fresh ammunition, filled the fuel tanks and carried out maintenance checks. Ignoring the explosions from the shell fire which fell on the forward slope of Cintheaux, the panzermen of Wittmann's group lay in the grass and smoked, unwinding and calming their nerves after the morning's battle.

All too soon, a runner from 'A' echelon reported that the Tigers were ready for action. The Hauptsturmführer looked round the circle of his men.

"Finish your food quickly, lads. We're off again." and when they had made ready gave the order to mount up.

"Mother Tiger to cubs. Start engines."

Quickly Wittmann carried out the standard checks on the inside of the fighting compartment. Everything was in its place, although he noted with renewed annoyance that because of the damned Command set the vehicle carried fewer rounds. Bending almost double he leaned forward to look at the fuel gauges - the tanks were full. At eye level was the rubber-covered mount of the freshly cleaned on-board periscope. That was another annoying feature of the tank's design. Its field of vision was limited. He could see nothing but the ground immediately ahead. Didn't the designers realise that a panzer commandant has to have an all-round view? The checks finished, it was time for him to determine what lay ahead.

Automatically, Wittmann checked the time on his wrist watch. When it came to writing a report on the day's fighting, timings were important. The Tiger moved slowly up the ridge at the back of Cintheaux village and he began to compose in his mind the opening lines of his report on the battle which lay ahead. "My group of four Tigers crossed the form-up line of the attack at 1409hrs, and moved forward to take hull-down positions on the reverse slope to the south of Cintheaux. I had laid down the start line as the crest of the ridge. From that point the attack proper would begin..."

The Hauptsturmführer grasped the pair of metal handles inside the turret and pulled himself up and through the hatch until he stood on the collapsible metal bucket seat. From that vantage point his vision was all-round. That was what a panzer commandant needed. To see everything. Over the standard radio set he spoke to the other panzer commandants to check that their machines were ready to go back into battle. They were.

"Everything in order? Right then. Marsch," he ordered.

Squeaking and rattling, the wide tracks on the Tigers carried them up the reverse slope of the ridge and towards its crest. Just below the crest, Wittmann halted the other vehicles while his own panzer crawled very, very slowly to a 'hull down' position. From the turret he surveyed the battlefield. Traversing his binoculars he could see on the west side of the N158 columns of black smoke which marked the victims of the Battalion's attack earlier that day. Smoke plumes closer to hand, on the east side of the road, identified those Canadian tanks which had crossed the road in an attempt to bypass Cintheaux and which the 'Hitler Youth' and his own group of panzers had attacked and destroyed. He noted a couple of Shermans knocked out and burning, only a few metres from a slit trench under a bocage hedge, in which a Grenadier machine gun team had dug in. These were freshly 'killed' victims.

Directly in front of him the Hauptsturmführer saw that in the village of Cramesnil, there were fires burning, still, and a great deal of confusion. The British armoured units in and around the place had clearly not yet recovered from the shock of being bombed from the air by their allies. The Tommy tankmen had still not taken up any sort of attack formation and their squadrons were still milling about seemingly aimlessly. To the right of Cramesnil village, at St Aignan, he could see the flashes of tank guns as British armoured regiments supported their own infantry battalions which were locked in battle with Waldmüller's Grenadiers. The line of advancing SS Hitler Youth was not more than a kilometre away from Wittmann, but even through binoculars he found it hard to distinguish them in their camouflaged jackets against the verdant Norman countryside in which they were fighting. Only the occasional flash as sunlight reflected from a weapon or from a piece of equipment indicated how far the Grenadier assault had reached. As Wittmann watched the battle he saw shell bursts erupt in front of the line of Waldmüller's soldiers. The Tommy artillery was laying down a curtain of fierce defensive fire. The Hauptsturmführer saw with a feeling of pride that the Grenadiers were advancing unflinchingly and without hesitation into the fury of the bombardment, and then vanished from his sight in the smoke and dust of the explosions.

Wittmann was convinced that he had nothing to fear from the British armour at St Aignan. The attack earlier that morning had shown him that the Tommy armoured regiments only had Shermans and he also knew that, except at close range, the 75s they carried could not penetrate his armour; certainly not at a kilometre's distance. But unknown to him, Fireflies, standard Shermans up-gunned and carrying a massive 17-pdr anti-tank gun, had been brought into the combat zone. Being ignorant of the fact that there were now enemy machines in the area which could 'kill' him at long range, Wittmann ran confidently through the options open to him. The enemy at St Aignan could be ignored for the time being. The group at Cramesnil were not yet ready to make their attack. There remained, then, the other major grouping on the far side of the N158. Satisfied with the quick check he had made, the Hauptsturmführer decided on his course of action. He would resume the attack against the enemy on the far side of the N158 and stop the Canadian armour from advancing towards Cintheaux. He climbed down into the battle compartment of his Tiger and picked up the microphone on the command set. In the earphones there was a loud crackling and whistling.

"Lot of static today, is there?" he asked the wireless operator.

"It's not static, Hauptsturmführer. It's the Tommies trying to jam our frequency. The interference has been getting worse since midday."

"We do have an alternative frequency, don't we?" And, noting the NCO's nodded assent, went on, "Tell the other operators to be ready to switch to the emergency frequency at my order, once I've issued battle orders," and switching the Command set to 'transmit' he began to brief the commandants of the four vehicles of his group.

"From Mother Tiger to all cubs. I am going to fire smoke over the ridge directly to our front. In a couple of minutes the screen will be thick enough to blanket us from our target, that is the Tommies on the far side of the N158. We shall move over the crest and take up position on the forward slope so that when the screen fades we shall be ready to open fire. Out."

He reached up, closed the hatch above his head and then spoke into the throat microphone. "Crew. You heard the orders I just gave. Gunner! Fire the smoke projectors." An opaque white curtain was soon drifting on the light air.

"Mother Tiger to cubs, Bodo and Caesar. Advance now." There was a wait for several minutes then he spoke again. "Cub Dora. Move now" and then to his own driver, Reimers. "Advance."

The Command Tiger, No 007, the last of the four, climbed the ridge, halted on the crest, dipped its bow and then began the long descent through the smoke which hid it and the other vehicles from the Canadians. "Hold tight," the driver warned. "Rough ground ahead." Then there was a bumping and a lurching as the Tigers passed over the ground cratered by the air raids of the past days. Wittmann clung onto the turret handles, the gunner hung onto the traversing gear and the loader grabbed the gun mechanism to prevent himself being flung about. The Tiger lumbered out of one crater and into another until, at last, it had passed out of the torn-up area. The approach march to battle was over. Wittmann unlocked the hatch cover and pulled himself upwards and into the open air, once again. Ahead of him were the three Tigers of his unit, cruising slowly towards the eastern side of the N158.

Chapter 19

"Mother Tiger to cubs. Slow down and then halt when we reach the Grenadiers. Get them on board quickly and let's get out of the area before the Yankee aircraft drop their shit..."

A few minutes' drive and Wittmann tapped with his foot on the driver's shoulder. At that signal Reimers brought the vehicle to a halt. The Grenadiers, loaded down with weapons, clambered on and hung onto the sides and turret of the Tiger.

"All set?" Wittmann asked and then spoke again to his cubs. "Panzer Marsch." The attack had begun.

The ground between the ridges of St Aignan and Cintheaux was undulating, offering the skilful panzer commandant a great deal of dead ground through which he could manoeuvre his vehicles to the objective, but only if he was up against a ground-based enemy. The British had a flying Command Post in the sky whose FOO saw everything and could switch the guns under his control swiftly from one target to another. Within minutes of Wittmann's panzer/panzergrenadier force moving forward, the vehicles were enshrouded by eruptions of earth and dust as a barrage of high explosive shells fell around them. The Hauptsturmführer's reaction to shells falling around his panzer was to increase speed. He knew that no gunner could reduce range as fast as the Tigers could move and the closer the armoured fighting vehicles drew to the enemy then the less intense was his artillery fire. In and out of the dead ground, using his countryman's skills to their best advantage, Wittmann brought his column of Grenadier-encrusted panzers up the steep rise leading towards St Aignan. He knew that the next minutes would be vital to the success of this initial attack. "Mother Tiger to cubs. Slow down and dismount the Grenadiers...Behind the ridge in front of us is a shallow valley. Tommy will be on the reverse slope. All cubs will fire three rounds of HE, fused for 500 metres so as to explode near the edge of the trees where the British infantry will be dug in. I expect the Tommies to send out their armour to meet us. We'll deal with them then. Ready, lads? Have you dropped your Grenadiers?" He listened for the messages of assent.

"Right - over the top." In seventh gear Reimers, the driver, flung the vehicle uphill and, as it breasted the crest, Wittmann noted with satisfaction that the picture which he saw before him was the one which he had anticipated seeing - on the reverse slope a line of slit trenches with the fresh-turned earth still clearly visible...and there in the depths of the concealing woods, but not completely hidden, the outlines of armoured fighting vehicles.

Wittmann's group of eighteen panzers formed up and adopted a shallow wedge formation with him as its point. "Don't stop your panzer to fire ," he ordered. "Fire while on the move. All cubs, three rounds of HE...Fire." The armoured arrow head thundered over the crest and headed downhill, clods of earth flying from the clattering tracks as the machines swayed from side to side in their careering course. True to form the British armour emerged from the trees and took post, halting in an extended line, waiting for the panzers to come within killing range. The Yeomanry knew that they were outgunned; that the 88's arming the Tigers outranged their own main armament and that Jerry tanks had thicker and stronger armour than that on their own Shermans and Stuarts. The only advantage they had was that they were firing from the halt; from a stable platform. The Jerry gunners could not aim accurately while on the move. With luck the Shermans might still give the Jerries a bloody nose.

Wittmann's eyes moved along the short line of British armour. Excellent. There were none of the dangerous Firefly tanks in the group and this meant that there was no danger to his panzers from the Sherman guns - except at point blank range, and he had no intention of coming in that close.

"Mother Tiger to cubs...Halt." and on the one side of the valley the long sinister wedge of Tigers and Panthers stood menacing, overlapping the British line. It was the Yeomanry who opened the battle with AP shot which either went wide or else struck the German machines but did not penetrate the thick armour and ricocheted off, breaking up into a shower of flashing lights, bright enough to be seen even on this clear and sunny day.

"Mother Tiger to cubs...We'll wait for the Grenadiers to catch up, then it's two rounds rapid AP and a charge to clear the Tommies from the woods." He turned round in the turret. Approaching at a jog trot came the SS infantry, in open order, ignoring the shell bursts and the solid shot that flew low over the field. As the Grenadiers passed his Tiger, Wittmann took up the advance again and with ear-splitting crashes the 88 fired its solid shot rounds at the Yeomanry tanks. Fires broke out here and there along the line, but the battle was not a one-sided affair. The British tankmen had learned that two AP shots fired in rapid succession and at the same spot could often damage even a Tiger tank. Cub Albert of Wittmann's group fell out with a broken track, the victim of just such a piece of skilful gunnery and on the right flank a couple of Panthers were immobile. But the German force was too powerful for the Yeomanry to resist for long and slowly the Shermans began to withdraw into the woods followed by the British infantry who pulled back to the village of St Aignan and began to prepare it for defence.

"Mother Tiger to cubs. Halt and secure…" Then, jumping from the Tiger's deck, Wittmann walked over to the officer leading the Grenadier group to discuss with him the next stage of the attack. So far the assault had gone extremely well despite the panzer losses, and even these would soon be made good. The Battalion's Workshop Company had already been advised and was sending up recovery vehicles to bring in the knocked-out machines. They could be operational again within a couple of hours.

Wittmann's immediate task was completed. He had carried the Grenadiers onto their start line and the time had come for him to lead one Company of the Battalion back to attack the enemy on the main road. The loss of Cub Albert had reduced his group to just his own Tiger and three others, but although they were few in number the skill of the crews of the 101st might yet be sufficient to halt the Canadian advance.

"All crews. Fuel and ammunition state, please."

The Hauptsturmführer was relieved that neither was needed. That way he would lose no time in having to restock but could switch his four panzers immediately towards the main road - and the second of the day's objectives. Hidden by the reverse slope of a slight rise Wittmann led his group on a diagonal line south-westwards from St Aignan towards Cintheaux but before the group reached the village Wittmann changed direction again and struck northwards so as to gain the N158. A stealthy climb brought the Tigers to just below the sky line. Climbing out of his vehicle the Hauptsturmführer walked up to the crest of the ridge, lay down on the short turf and studied the armoured mass of Canadian tanks on the far side of the main road. They still seemed to be in a state of confusion. Their efforts were uncoordinated. He could see no sign of any support groups with them; nothing but a mass of tanks driving around, seemingly aimlessly. Then he spotted the reason for that confusion. He made out the anti-tank gunners of the Hitler Youth, hidden in storks of corn and taking a heavy toll of the Shermans. Any tanks which did manage to cross the road, intending to drive up it towards Cintheaux, were being stalked, attacked and destroyed by Grenadier teams using panzerfausts. There was keen competition among the SS infantry to 'kill' the enemy tanks - each one destroyed counted towards the gold close-combat arm badge. Another, and probably greater inducement, was the seven days' home leave which accompanied the award.

Despite the actions of the panzerfaust teams and the anti-tank gunners some Shermans had established a bridgehead to the north of Gaumesnil. The force was still quite small, a squadron of Shermans and some armoured personnel carriers but clearly the intention was to gain touch with the other Tommy armour on the ridge. Wittmann decided that a short, sharp intervention would smash the bridgehead group. Then he would take his panzers back to 'A' echelon to rearm and refuel before moving off to attack the third objective of the day; the Cramesnil group.

"Mother Tiger to cubs. At 11 o'clock, about 600 metres from us there is an enemy group, a bridgehead on the east side of the N158. We shall destroy that group. It includes APCs and when we hit them the Tommy infantry will bail out - so machine gunners, you too will have plenty of targets to fire at. Right. Load up with AP. All cubs, move to take hull-down positions along the ridge."

The four vehicles of Wittmann's group moved slowly and carefully up the slope to line the reverse slope so that only their turrets showed above the crest. The long barrels of the 88s began to swing towards the 11. o'clock position. The Hauptsturmführer detailed the first target for each of his cubs and as he spoke the turrets swung, more slowly now, to bring the 88s to bear upon the unsuspecting Canadian tanks which were sorting themselves into order on the eastern side of the main road. The main enemy force was a squadron of Sherbrookes, escorting two companies of the Grenadier Guards of Canada, the reconnaissance unit of 4th Canadian Armoured Division.

"Report when on." Wittmann stood on the bucket seat in the turret watching the enemy machines. More and more Shermans were crossing from the western side of the road to join the Sherbrooke group. "On, on, on." came the succession of reports. "Fire!" and the solid shot of the first salvo struck four of the Canadian vehicles and destroyed them. Wittmann selected four fresh targets. Another salvo smashed the APCs and then, increasing the range, the Tiger group opened fire upon the tank squadrons now reaching the eastern side of the N158.

Surprise had been total. The Canadians, with their attention concentrated on the anti-tank gunners and the panzerfaust teams, had not reckoned with an enemy more than a kilometre distant. Then, at Wittmann's command, over the crest of the ridge lumbered the four

Tigers and charged downhill towards the Sherbrookes and the Grenadier Guards. Bravery is a fine thing. The ability to act decisively at times of great danger is a positive attribute in a commander and the Sherbrooke Commanding Officer was a decisive leader. He decided to void the field and withdraw back across the N158, hoping to entice the Tigers to where the Canadian guns on the eastern side of the road could destroy them.

"Sunray here. All runners. Stand fast until the Guards have escaped then pull back and rendezvous at RHQ. I'll try to raise our Gunner chums in the flying OP to see if they can hold those Tigers while we pull out."

The familiar fountains of earth were soon rising and falling around the Tigers as the observer in the shufti-kite, the eye in the sky, concentrated the fire of three regiments of artillery onto Wittmann's group. Once again the Hauptsturmführer's reaction was to increase speed - to pass quickly through the barrage and to engage the enemy on the far side of the shell explosions. On that far side there was now only a handful of Sherbrooke tanks still in action and their fire concentrated upon the lead Tiger, Wittmann's. The Sherman shells struck and although they did not penetrate and 'kill' the panzer the jarring impact not only dazed Wittmann's crew but struck off, from inside of the vehicle, shards of metal which flew, razor sharp, around the cordite-reeking fighting compartment. Wagner, the layer, squinting through his gun sight, saw a Sherman loom up. It was that of the Sherbrooke Colonel. As he pressed the firing button the Tiger lurched into a crater so that the shot struck low, hitting the Sherbrooke's track but not killing the machine. Another Sherman was now in his sights. Wagner fired and destroyed the Squadron leader's machine. Halted and trading shot for shot with Wittmann's Tiger another Sherman fired round after round to cover the withdrawal from the battlefield of the CO's crippled tank. As the crippled Sherman struggled back the Colonel heard behind him the familiar 'whoofing' sound of a Sherman 'brewing up' and turned to see who had bought it. It was the tank which had been covering him. The crew had paid with their lives for their act of heroism.

Soon the Tigers stood on the ground where the Sherbrooke tanks had set up their bridgehead. From the turret of his panzer Wittmann looked towards the enemy grouping around Cramesnil. The scene was still one of confusion. He could risk leaving the battlefield to obtain fresh supplies.

"Mother Tiger to cubs. Rendezvous at Cintheaux for fuel and

ammunition. Are there any casualties to report?"

One after the other the cubs reported to Wittmann that all was well. His own crew had suffered some damage as a result of enemy shell strikes. One shot which had hit close to the radio set had concussed Hirschel, the radio operator, and he changed places with the co-driver. Then Tiger 007 rolled back along the bocage hedge to 'A' echelon at Cintheaux to find the village was under bombardment. The Allies, determined to break through the German line, were laying down a long and sustained artillery barrage. A few houses in the village had escaped damage in the air raids of the previous days, but in the fury of the present shellfire they had all been smashed into rubble. Cintheaux had been reduced to a pile of rubble, smelling strongly of the smoke from the fires which raged within.

Chapter 20

The crews and vehicles of No 3 Troop of the Northampton Yeomanry's A Squadron were dispersed among the trees of a large, triangular piece of woodland to the south of St Aignan. The poncey Sassenach tankmen and their bloody noisy vehicles were both resented by the Infantry Companies of 1st Black Watch who had dug their slit trenches just in front of the trees. The armour was unwelcome. Everyone knew that the presence of tanks brought down shit. It happened all the time. At intervals a tank would come lumbering through the trees, would drive as far forward as the slit trenches and then fire off four or five shells. Then the bloody tank would pull back into cover but the German gunners would have seen and reported its movement and a couple of minutes later a barrage of shells would fall around the slit trenches of the unprotected infantry. Tankmen and their stinking vehicles were a sodding nuisance and the attitude of the Royal Highlanders made the Yeomen very aware that the Jocks didn't want them around. If only, if only, the Yeoman thought, there was something to show the Black Watch what they could do. And then, as if in answer to their unspoken prayer, the men of No 3 Troop on watching duty in the orchard, saw Wittmann's column of four Tigers driving across their front. This was a dream target. The Tigers were on the east side of the N158, moving slowly northwards, spaced at intervals and silhouetted against the wall of smoke. Through binoculars the Yeomanry NCO could see that the long 88s were not pointed towards St Aignan but towards the main road and the Canadians. Wittmann, confident that the Tommy tank regiments around St Aignan could not destroy him, had no hesitation in crossing their front; flaunting his invulnerability. Nevertheless he felt unease. There was an odd feeling at the back of his mind, a sixth sense warning him that some sort of danger threatened from the Shermans in St Aignan. What that danger might be, he did not know, but the feeling of disquiet was there. He shouted above the jamming which he could hear in the earphones on the Command set.

"Mother Tiger to cub Dora. Drop back. Drop back. I need flank protection. Over."

"Cub Dora to Mother Tiger. Complying. Out," and Dora halted until the Hauptsturmführer's panzer had drawn level with it. Then it took up position slightly behind and on the right flank of Panzer 007. Wittmann picked up the Command set microphone again but this time the earphones were filled with a cacophony of raucous whistling, singing and long sentences in fast-spoken English as well as the usual loud crackling static. He bent down towards the wireless operator, pointed at the earphones and in an interrogative gesture raised his shoulders. "The jamming's getting worse," the wireless operator mouthed in reply.

"Tell the cubs to go over to the alternative frequency and warn Dora to watch St Aignan carefully." The wireless operator moved the dials and then reported that the alternative frequency was also jammed. Both frequencies, he told Wittmann, were so badly affected that no wireless communication between the vehicles of his group was possible. The Hauptsturmführer was annoyed at this complication. He couldn't really give hand signals. The other commandants would not expect to see them in the middle of an action. His cubs would have to fight the battle without his direct control. It wouldn't be the first time and it had always worked in Russia. Why not here in Normandy ?

From the orchard near St Aignan, A Squadron Commander and his second in command watched the Tigers calmly driving across the Yeomanry front.

"Cheeky bastards, flaunting themselves like that" said the Commander. "I reckon their range as about 1200 yards. What do you think, Tom?"

"At the moment, yes, but pretty soon, if they maintain present speed and direction, in a couple of minutes they should be only 800 yards away. Then they'll be in killing range of the 17-pdrs in the Fireflies. I'll get one of them to come forward and we'll take that little lot out."

The Squadron Commander agreed. "OK, Tom. Tell the other Sherman crews to hold their fire until the Firefly has engaged the targets. Then they can all have a go."

Minutes later and the second in command stood beside the Firefly which had been ordered forward and looked at the huge gun projecting from its turret. His mind was working on the probabilities which could result when he opened fire. The enemy had four Tigers, each armed with an 88 which could kill at 1000 yards. He had only one Firefly with a 17 pdr which could penetrate a Tiger's armour at 800 yards so the Firefly would have to kill one of the enemy machines and pull back into cover before the other Tigers could swing their turrets and engage it. Taking advantage of whatever situation developed, the Firefly could come out, fire another 'killing' shot and then pull back again into the shade of the trees. It should work. He explained to the Firefly commander what he wanted done.

"Ready, Sergeant?"

"Yes, Sir."

"Then fire at will." The Firefly shuddered as the first round crashed out, then shook again and this time more violently as the second round was fired.

A flash of light, magnesium bright, flying out of the orchard to the south of St Aignan, caught Wittmann's eye. A second brilliant flash held his attention completely. Then he saw two glowing white balls showing bright against the dark green of the trees. The first ball growing larger in size and seemingly more bright, swung toward cub Dora and struck her in the side. There was a crashing detonation. Pieces of her armour began to fly off but before they had gone far the second glowing ball hit the stricken machine. A greyish-black cloud erupted out of the turret and then that dark cloud was suddenly red-streaked as Dora burst into flames.

Instinctively, Wittmann had ordered the turret of 007 to be traversed towards the aggressive enemy. He checked through his binoculars and felt his heart sink. His sixth sense had been right. He and his cubs were in terrible danger. The enormous main armament which he could see through his field glasses told him that the enemy machine was a Firefly. He cursed himself for not having thought that this Tommy unit might have one or more on its establishment. How could he have ignored so obvious a consideration? How could he have been so neglectful of flank protection, of not having taken precautions, of having cruised across the enemy's front in so casual a manner? He closed his mind to these negative thoughts. The need to take action was immediate and needed all his concentration.

"Driver: Halt." Then to the gunners. "Main armament. Target : tank. Location: 2 o'clock. Distance 800 metres. Load with armour piercing. Fire when on."

Within seconds the first of three 88mm shells was flying towards the Firefly, now pulling back into cover. The solid shot projectiles glistening in the sunlight, missed the tank and vanished into the trees. Inside the concealing dark of the orchard the Firefly crew talked excitedly of the 'kill'.

"Give your gunner my congratulations, Sergeant," said the Squadron 2 i/c. "Now, move out again and attack the rear Tiger. The rest of the Troop will open fire on the other pair of vehicles and create a diversion to cover you."

For a second time the Firefly rolled slowly forward through the trees, emerged briefly from cover and rolled to a halt. A single shot crashed out and the tank reversed back into the concealing shade. Wittmann and his gun layer had both seen the enemy vehicle emerge. "Fire" and the sulphurous cloud which poured from the muzzle of the 88 hid the bright flash that left that of the Firefly. Seconds later its armour piercing shell had struck 007, and penetrating between the turret and the hull in a single second killed the Tiger. The solid shot had penetrated the Tiger's side armour but, lacking the power to punch an exit hole, ricocheted at lightning speed around the panzer's fighting compartment and killed all whom it touched. The first to die was the gunner. The whizzing, red hot projectile struck him before he was even aware that the Tiger had been hit and in its careering course the steel shot mashed his torso into bloody pulp. The loader-operator died in the same fashion leaving undamaged only the fingers of his severed right hand fixed on the dial of the Command set. Reimers, the driver, felt the Tiger shake violently as the enemy shell struck home and was aware of a wet warmth which flooded across his shoulders and neck. Completely disorientated by the force of the impact, his reactions were slow but then came the realisation that the hot fluid which was cascading onto the vehicle's controls was blood. Still not completely aware of the situation, nor of the danger he was in, he stayed for a second or two in the driving seat before making his escape from the Tiger.

By comparison, the reactions of the co-driver, Hirschel, were lightning fast. Almost as if he had been anticipating the shell-strike, at the moment when it came he threw himself forward from his seat to undo the bow escape hatch. The Tiger's violent shuddering flung him through the forward hatch and onto the grass. He lay on the earth, dazed with concussion, waiting until he could summon up energy enough to crawl away from the stricken machine. He could hear nothing. Temporarily he was deafened, but it had happened before as a result of other shell strikes in other battles and he knew the deafness would soon pass. There was also a taste of blood in his mouth. Well, that was not unusual, either. He must have banged his face on something when he bailed out. Instinctively he touched his ears to make sure they were still there and then looked at his hands. Both palms were covered with blood. Concussion, he thought. No wonder I can hear nothing. That probably accounts for the blood in my mouth, was his next thought. He looked around. Was he the only crew member to have got out? If so, then he had better go back to the panzer and try to rescue the others. Then he saw Reimers, blood-covered but still moving well, come round the bow of the Tiger.

"The others...?" he began.

Reimers gestured towards his panzer jacket. "All dead..." Hirschel lip-read his words and then asked through the blood that was filling his mouth.

"The CO?"

Wittmann had been flung forward by the impact and had struck his head on the turret machine gun mount. Briefly he was unconscious and, when he came round, was vaguely aware that something had happened to his left leg. It ached with a dull, persistent throbbing. He clutched the throat microphone. "Crew, crew. Bail out," he ordered and although dazed noted that nobody had acknowledged the order. Dully, and without emotion, his mind accepted that all the other crew members must be dead. Now he had to get himself out of the Tiger before it began to burn. He levered himself up using his hands and arms until his upper thighs were level with the turret rim, sat on the wide metal ring and tried to swing his legs over it. Only the right leg responded. Still without emotion he accepted that his left leg must have been broken. He took a deep breath, placed his hands under his left leg and pulled it up over the rim. The calf was pouring blood. It didn't seem to be too bad a wound. I'm lucky, he thought, not to have lost both legs when the Tommy shot hit us. Taking a second deep breath, he jumped from the after deck of the Tiger and landed awkwardly. His right leg began to buckle under him and he saved himself from falling only by instinctively putting all his weight on the left leg. Blood spurted from the severed veins but there was still no acute pain. This was only a temporary relief. He knew that terrible pain would set in once the initial shock had worn off. Through the daze of concussion he saw Reimers and Hirschel watching him. Their faces were concerned and Wittmann noted that the driver's tunic was drenched with blood.

"Are you badly hurt, Reimers?"

"Not at all, Hauptsturmführer. Not even a scratch. It's the gunners' blood. They're both dead. Hirschel has very severe concussion. He's bleeding from the ears and mouth. The wireless operator must also be dead. But you've been hit "

"Just a flesh wound, I think, but let's get away from here. The Tiger will go up any second now. I'm sorry but you and Hirschel will have to support me. I can't walk. Take me as far as the road. There's a section of Waldmüller's Grenadiers in position there. They are certain to have a medical orderly with them. He can put a tourniquet on my leg. Let's get away from here quickly."

The three survivors of 007 moved slowly towards the bocage hedge but had barely covered twenty paces when, from inside the Tiger, a violent explosion blew off the heavy turret and gun. From out of the fire blazing in the hull, multi-coloured flares, the vehicle's Very lights as well as green, red and white tracer rounds, climbed into the afternoon sky.

Klein, commandant of Tiger Bodo, felt the heat from the explosion before he heard the roar of the detonation. Turning round in the turret he saw two of Wittmann's crew carrying their commander's body between them. This was an emergency which required drastic action. He spoke to his crews.

"The CO needs help. All out of the Tiger."

The crew of Bodo emerged from their hatches and ran towards Reimers and Hirschel. They ran across the grass in a tight little group and, when a 75mm shell from one of A Squadron's Shermans burst among them, the Bodo crew died in a tight little group. Tiger Caesar, which had been firing at the British vehicles hidden in the orchard, was now the target for all A Squadron's guns and, hit by the Firefly's, shells she began to burn. The death of that Tiger cub marked the end of Wittmann's Command.

On the rim of a slit trench dug below the hedge, Reimers and Hirschel laid down their officer's unconscious body. Deftly, Hirschel tied a tourniquet around the wounded leg between the knee and the calf. The pain of that sudden constriction shocked the Hauptsturmführer back into awareness. He felt sick with pain.

"Give me a drink, please, Reimers, and then find me some sort of weapon."

He drank from Reimers' water bottle and within seconds had regained full command of himself.

"Leave me here," he ordered. "You make your way back to Cintheaux. Send back a medical orderly. You must get back into action as soon as you can. Every crewman is needed."

Reimers handed his commander an MP 40 and a full magazine. "I found these in the slit trench. There's a couple of dead Grenadiers in it as well as an MG42, but you'd never manage to hold a machine gun in your condition."

"Right, lads, away you go." Awkwardly, Wittmann eased himself round to see them leave. There was a sudden loud noise close by and he turned grunting with the effort to see what had caused it. The machine pistol was in his hands, loaded and cocked. The last things that Michael Wittmann saw in this life were men of a patrol from the Sherbrookes pushing their way through the hedge along the side of the road. They halted and stood facing him. The Canadians had learned quickly that speed of reaction was the key to survival on the battlefield. They saw before them a black uniformed panzer officer with a Schmeisser machine pistol in his hand. Instinctively and without hesitation they opened fire. The impact of the Sten gun bullets fired at so close a range knocked the Hauptsturmführer backwards. As he fell the grip of his dying fingers pressed the machine pistol's trigger and a stream of bullets flew into the air. The Sherbrookes fired again and then shot down Reimers and Hirschel as they came racing back to help their Commander.

Reimers fell forward into the trench and landed, spread-eagled, on top of the MG42 and the corpses of a two-man Grenadier machine gun team. Hirschel fell backwards, twitching in his death throes. Wittmann lay on his back, his head dangling over the rim of the slit trench. Sergeant Hampton of the Sherbrookes gave a curt order.

"Chuck them in the slit trench and let's get back to RHQ."

The crash of a salvo of shells falling close by gave urgency to the Sherbrookes' work. This was no time to search the bodies for identification or to take off their identity discs. As two men of the patrol swung Wittmann's corpse ready to throw it into the slit trench which was now a grave, Lance-Corporal Milligan noticed the Knight's Cross around the dead man's neck.

"Well, he won't need that where he's gone," he rationalised, tore the cross and ribbon away and stuffed them in his pocket. The Hauptsturmführer's corpse landed face down in the trench. Hirschel's body followed. The shellfire crashed closer to the patrol. It was time to go and the Sherbrookes moved quickly away from the area.

"That Kraut with the Iron Cross," began Lance-Corporal Milligan. "I could feel that his leg was hanging by a thread"

"Bugger that Kraut and his leg," retorted Hampton. "Let's concentrate on getting back." And the patrol moved swiftly up the bocage hedge which ran along the eastern side of the N158.

A Squadron had at first been puzzled that the lead Tiger, cub Bodo, had not opened fire. Then the British tank crews had seen its crew leap from their machine and run, only to see them disappear in a shell burst. The Squadron's 2 i/c had watched dispassionately through his binoculars as 007's survivors struggled towards the road, had seen the Canadian patrol come through the hedge and shoot the German Tiger crew. Them or us, he thought. The Captain checked his watch.

It was 1255hrs. At this point the reader will note that there is a difference in the times given in this account of the battle. When Wittmann checked his watch before crossing the start line it had been 1409hrs. The Yeomanry Captain's watch at the end of the action read only 1255hrs. The explanation is simple. We Germans worked on Berlin time which was two hours ahead of British Time.

The Captain's watch showed 1255hrs. At this time, back in the UK he thought, we'd be having gin and tonics, but his pleasant reminiscence was cut short.

"Column of German tanks, twenty plus, moving across the Squadron's front from left to right," reported a sentry. "Range about 1200 yards."

The 2 i/c deployed his Troop to meet the new challenge. It had been a bastard of a day and it wasn't really afternoon yet. God knows what would happen when that new lot of Jerry armour came into action. Thank God, the Poles would be coming through in about 40 minutes and would take up the running. Those bloody Hitler Youth sods fight like fanatics, he thought. Well, the Poles may have seen little action yet, but they'll soon teach Hitler's Youths a thing or two. Meanwhile, there was the War Diary to be written up. It would make a very readable entry:

"1232hrs, Column of four Tigers crossed the Squadron's front. Fire was opened by a Firefly with the following results.

1240hrs. The Tiger at the rear of the column knocked-out and burning.

1247hrs. The Tiger in front of the burning one was hit and blew up.

1252hrs. The Tiger leading the column was knocked out and 'brewed up'.

One Tiger was abandoned by its crew."

Yes, three Tigers in twelve minutes. Very impressive gunnery, thought the Squadron 2 i/c.

~

Wittmann was dead. We know it now. Just as we now know what we had all thought, that he died to the sound of battle. He had died with the smell of gunsmoke in his nostrils and with a gun in his hands. The bodies in the slit trench could not have been left long uncovered. Shell fire would have scattered the first earth over them and then, perhaps, a tank crashing through the hedge and passing close by, might have collapsed the trench's earthen walls leaving nothing to indicate that the spot was a grave, holding five of our dead comrades.

For forty years the Norman soil had held a secret which only the persistence of our group had unlocked and which had resolved the fate of Michael Wittmann and his crew, particularly Reimers and Hirschel. For decades they had been registered as 'missing in action', but we had found their grave. It was done. The last service to our Commanding Officer was nearly completed. There remained now only the official interment. And when considering this, I began to have doubts.

Chapter 21

On 10th August, two days after we had found our Commanding Officer's body, the representatives of the German War Graves Commission arrived at the inn in which we were staying. They greeted Beck, who was their colleague in the Commission, and then asked whether we would all be going to the site that day. What a stupid question! Of course we would be going. Today would mark the end of our quest and we wanted to be there at its end. The motor coach brought us along the N158 and stopped north of Gaumesnil. Although it was not yet 1000hrs it was another stifling hot day and the heat seemed to be reflected off the open fields. While Beck and the officers of the Commission began their work I looked at the countryside over which we had fought decades before. We had made so many visits to this area looking for our young commander and, now that we had found him, we would probably never ever visit Normandy again. Very little remained of the traditional Norman fields. Modern agricultural methods had swept away the constricting, almost claustrophobic, hedges and orchards among which we had fought. Only the shape of the ground could not be changed and I looked towards the ridge on which stood the villages of St Aignan and Cramesnil.

Just in front of St Aignan there had been extensive woods near which Wittmann and his crew had fought on their last day of battle. Those woodlands had been cut back now and only part of the forest was the same as I remembered it. That part was the triangular section into which Waldmüller's Battle Group of 25th SS Panzergrenadier Regiment had fought its way. That small section of forest and the ravine to the south-east of St Aignan were among the few - the very few - landmarks that I recognised. A loud voice broke my reverie. It was the leader of the War Graves Commission asking Beck a question.

"This is the lot then, Beck? The bones, uniform pieces and the pistol?"

"Yes, except for the identity discs. I have them with me now."

"Let me have them, please. None was attached to a particular body, was it ?"

"No. They were all found in the grave. What happens now?" Beck was asking that question more for our benefit than for his own.

The man from the Commission told us that the site was clearly a battlefield grave, holding five German soldiers. That number of skulls had been found. The uniform fragments identified the dead men as having been SS and the identity discs showed that three of the fallen comrades had been of 101st Panzer Battalion. Forensic examination to establish identity would be required but this would not take more than a week. By the end of August the formal interment of our dead comrades would take place in La Cambe military cemetery.

It must have come as a surprise to the others of our group when I announced that I would not be returning to Normandy to attend the formal burial in La Cambe. Angry voices demanded to know why.

"Why? Why?"

I asked. "Isn't it obvious ? Wittmann died on this field. This is his grave, a soldier's grave on the field where he gained glory and met death. That other cemetery at La Cambe is doubtless well laid out and orderly, but Wittmann will not be there. His bones may be buried there but the spirit of our commander is here in this field, and will be here for ever." There was an embarrassed silence, then some muttering and finally it was Brodski who spoke and he seemed to speak for us all.

"This, comrades, is the place where we say farewell to our Commander." He turned to me. "Of course you are correct. I shall not be going, either, to La Cambe."

We looked down at the plastic sheet lying on the grass. On it was a collection of bones, skulls and pieces of uniform. We shared a deep sadness as we looked at the remains of our comrades How young they had all been. How full of life and filled with a sense of adventure.

There was a long, deep and heavy silence then out of that silence Brodski began to sing the Panzerlied - the anthem of the German armoured troops.

Our song.

"*Ob's stürmt oder schneit, ob die Sonne uns lacht…*" His voice was shaky to begin with…he too, felt the emotion of the moment. Then other voices joined in and then we were all singing, the tears coursing, unchecked, down our faces. Our voices no longer held the weak and uncertain tones of old men. Somehow, by some strange chemistry, they had become once again, young men's voices. The song ended. We stood a little breathless in the shattering heat but then Hartmann from a Grenadier Battalion of the 12th SS Division started with a new song.

"*Wenn alle untreu werden…*" It was the SS anthem. Not for decades had we dared to sing that song in public. But today, what did we care if the trendy Lefties described us as unrepentant Nazis. This was not rampant Nazism. No!! We were saying farewell to comrades who had fallen in battle when those songs were still sung with hope and with conviction. Now, today, we were saying farewell without flags, bands or banners, but with the simple dignity of front-line soldiers.

When the song ended, Brodski held up his hand. "No more, comrades." He was, perhaps, afraid that we might begin singing even more provocative songs. He called us to attention and then ordered. "Remove head-dress." The officials of the War Graves Commission reverently folded the plastic sheet around the skeleton pieces and carried them to their Mercedes.

"Salute," and our hands rose to pay the final compliment to the young commander. The Mercedes moved off and roared away up the N158 towards Caen, the city where we had first met Wittmann. On its long journey it would pass Villers-Bocage where he had scored his greatest triumph on the Western Front and then it would head eastwards, taking Wittmann home to Germany for autopsy. Soon he would come back again to rest among our German dead in La Cambe cemetery. The car disappeared up the road in a small cloud of dust.

Michael Wittmann had left the battlefield in which he had rested for four decades and I, for one, felt suddenly that I was a very old man.